THE
Reluctant
Deckhand

Jan Padgett

illustrated by Amanda Forbis

Pacific Educational Press
Vancouver Canada

Published by Pacific Educational Press
Faculty of Education, University of British Columbia
Vancouver, Canada V6T 1Z4
Telephone (604) 822-5385
Facsimile (604) 822-6603

The publisher would like to acknowledge the contributions of the Department of Canadian Heritage and the Canada Council towards its publishing program.

A special thank-you to Dr. Jay Powell of the Museum of Anthropology at the University of British Columbia for his advice on the use of Kwak'wala words and references to Kwakiutl customs.

Canadian Cataloguing in Publication Data

Padgett, Jan, 1946-
　The reluctant deckhand

　ISBN 1-895766-01-X

　I. Forbis, Amanda. II. Title.
PS8581.A33R4 1995　　　jC813'.54　　　C95-910757-6
PZ7.P32Re 1995

Editing by Carolyn Sale
Design by Warren Clark
Printed and bound in Canada

10 9 8 7 6 5 4 3 2

To the memory of my mother,
Florence Padgett, who instilled in me
a respect for the sea and a love for the shore,
and to my daughters, Caitlin and Tegan,
who carry that love forward.
And for daughters and mothers everywhere,
no matter how far from shore.

Contents

Author's Acknowledgements

Tess's story would not have grown up to become a film and a book without the support of two special friends, Pat Taylor and Sue Milligan. Both were there at the beginning and stuck with me throughout the years it has taken to complete this project. Pat always believed I could do it; her insights were invaluable and her encouragement always got me through the rough spots. Sue shared with me her expertise and knowledge of fishing and the coast we both love so much. Many happy hours were spent with her on her classic live-hold fish boat, the *Henry Bay*, and I will treasure those memories.

My thanks to Catherine Edwards, at Pacific Educational Press, for coming on board the project, and to the editor, Carolyn Sale, for asking for more.

And to Susan Jean, the biggest thanks of all.

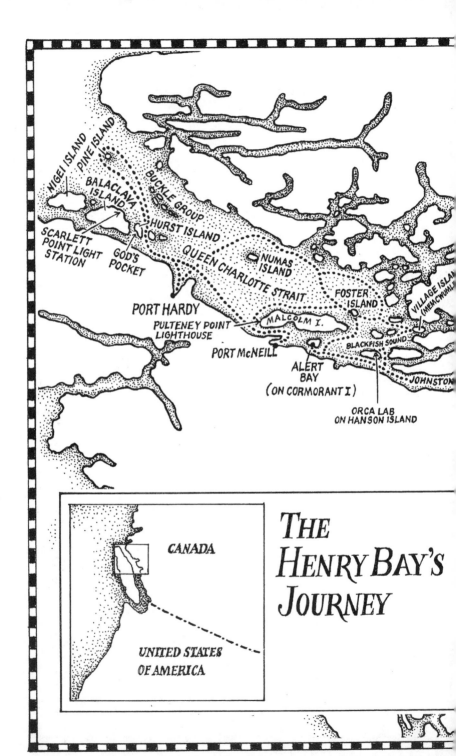

THE
HENRY BAY'S
JOURNEY

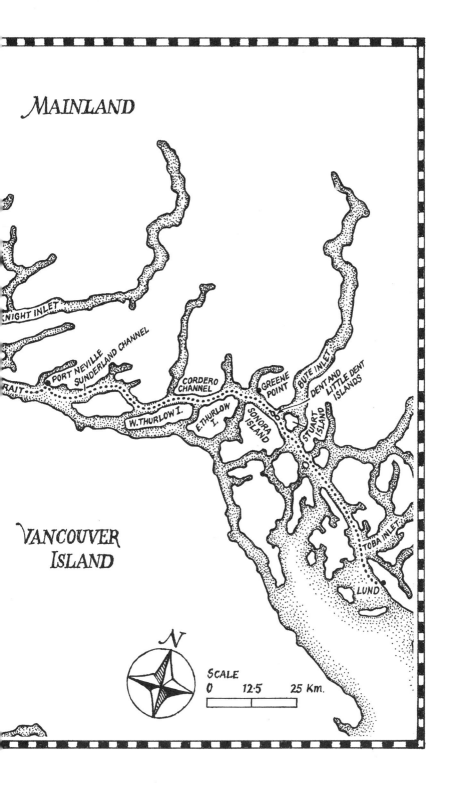

1

Time to Go

"Why do I have to?" asked Tess, her blue eyes dark with anger.

"Tess, we've been through this a hundred times," said her mother, Sue.

"But, Mom, I don't want to go!" said Tess, turning away. Sue stood looking at her daughter's back. With a sigh, she picked up a box of groceries and went into the wheelhouse.

Tess slumped on top of the icebox of their fish boat, the *Henry Bay*. She swung her legs back and forth, banging her heels against the side of the empty box. The loud hollow thud beat out a rhythm. Thump, bump. Thump, bump. Have to go. Have to go. Thump, bump.

The box would soon be full of ice-chips that would keep the fish fresh after they had been caught. Just thinking about it made her stomach tighten into a knot.

She looked out from the harbour at Lund to the Strait of Georgia. Inside the breakwater it was sheltered, safe, and calm. But beyond, in the middle of the channel, a southeaster was pushing up white-capped waves. The clouds were dark and heavy. Tess sighed, wishing it could have been sunny on the day they had to leave. If it had been sunny and calm she might have felt excited. Instead, she just felt scared.

Tess looked back up the road that led past the big white hotel with its restaurant and general store. The road was empty. Where was Candice? Last night Candice had promised Tess that even though they were leaving early in the morning she would come to the dock to say goodbye. It was hard for Tess to imagine a whole summer without her best friend. What was she going to do?

A few other people were down on the docks, tending their fish boats. Beside them, the *Henry Bay* gleamed with a new coat of paint. The cabin was white, with a stripe of orange and yellow just below the roof. The hull was a dark forest green, with a yellow water line and a red-brown bottom. Sue had used gold paint to letter the name *Henry Bay* on each side of the bow. She had added a golden dolphin, leaping from the Y, for good luck. Sue assured Tess they would see lots of dolphins in the more northern fishing waters where they were headed. Tess had been excited thinking about that. But now the time had come to leave, and Tess was filled with a sense of dread.

All the while that Tess had been growing up, she had heard stories of her mother's fishing adventures up north. Before Tess was born, her mother had taken her fish boat up to the north end of Vancouver Island where the cold waters of the Pacific Ocean pushed into Johnstone Strait. Although the conditions were harder, the water rougher with ocean swells and tidal currents, and the wind cold and wet as it blew in off the open sea, it was an area full of fish. And full of adventures and eccentric characters, from what Tess had heard. Her mother loved it all, but Tess thought it sounded too wild and scary for her.

Her mother had stopped fishing for the first three years of Tess's life. But they were never far from the sea. Their little yellow house was perched on the rocky point at the south end of the harbour at Lund. From her bedroom, Tess could watch the fish boats and freighters, sailboats and tugs travelling up and down the strait.

Sue took jobs on shore to be close to her daughter. She worked in the general store and the post office, and leased the *Henry Bay* to a friend to use. But Sue loved to fish. She loved the independence, freedom, and adventure it offered as well as the hard work. And she was good at it. She knew the winds and the tides, and she was always careful not to overfish an area. So she started fishing again. At first, she went out only on day trips but as Tess grew older, Sue went out on longer trips, leaving Tess to stay with Candice and her mother.

Even though Sue was happy to be fishing again, she always talked about wanting to go back up north, past the northern end of Johnstone Strait to the more exposed waters beyond. Her face would light up and her voice, usually low and husky, would rise in pitch as she described orcas rubbing along the rocky shelves of the shore, dolphins moving through the bow waves, and eagles by the dozen waiting for salmon to return to the streams. Paul the whale watcher, God's Pocket, Anne and Leslie at the lighthouse—these names had bounced around in Tess's head for as long as she could remember. They would go north together, her mother had said, when Tess was old enough. Tess used to ask her when that would be. The answer was always the same: "We'll know when the time comes."

Well, the time had come. Tess was now ten. She had spent time last summer helping her mother on the boat, fishing close to home in the Strait of Georgia. They fished in sheltered places where the water was calm in the summer, the air warm and soft, and the evenings long and gentle. The dusk would slowly gather as the boat tugged quietly at anchor.

These fishing trips had made the upper Strait of Georgia seem like a big backyard to Tess. She knew what was around every rocky point and each little island. The swimming holes, the sandy bays, the safe anchorages were all familiar to her. But this year Sue was satisfied that Tess was old enough to spend the whole summer up north with her.

At first Tess had felt excited and proud to be going. But as the day of departure grew closer, she felt more and more anxious. It was hard to talk to Mom about it. Her mother was so excited to be going and so busy fixing up the boat that she didn't seem to hear anything Tess said.

During the day, Tess's fears seemed silly to her. It was only as she lay in bed at night that the worries closed in on her. What if the swells made her seasick all the time? What if it was always cold and wet and rough? And what about the rapids and the tidal currents that they would have to go through, the unknown reefs and rocks? She had seen a chart of the west coast, dotted with sinking ships that marked the locations of boat wrecks. There were hundreds of them. What if something happened to her, or worse even, to her mom? She didn't know anyone up there. Who would help her?

And what kind of summer holiday would it be without Candice? Who would she play with, and when? She thought of all the hours they had spent together riding their bikes along shady dirt roads and exploring the beach, swimming in the clear water and then flopping down, cool and wet, to soak up the heat of the hot smooth rocks. She thought of the days spent at the neighbour's farm, the sweet smell of the horses, and the gentle sound as they munched the grass. That, to Tess, was summer.

"Tess." Sue's voice crashed into her thoughts. "Tess." She called again from the wheelhouse where she was busy putting food and supplies into the little storage cupboards.

Tess did not answer. The only sound was the thump of her gumboots.

Sue stuck her head out of the top of the double Dutch door. Her cheeks were flushed from working. She pushed back a strand of fuzzy blonde hair that had sprung loose from her hairband. She frowned, and took a deep breath. Then she said, in as cheery a voice as she could, "Come on, Tess. Where's my number one helper?"

Tess did not turn. She hunched her shoulders and continued staring out to sea. Sue hesitated.

"Tess, you know we have to leave as soon as possible to get through the rapids by the Dent Islands and at Greene Point. We have to hit them at slack tide. And we still have these last few things to stow."

Tess raised her head and turned to look at her. "You know I get seasick when it's rough," she said.

"It's not that bad up there," Sue replied.

"But why do I have to go?"

Sue rolled her eyes. She took a deep breath and blew the air out through her mouth. She said softly, "Tess, we've been over this again and again. Fishing is what I do, and there are more fish up north. I want to go north and I want to take you with me. And I'm sure you'll like it."

Tess continued to glare at her mom. "Why don't I have any choice?"

"Because I don't want to spend the whole summer without you. Two months away is too long. I know it's hard being away from home and your friends, but I don't want to leave you behind." Sue paused and then grinned. "This may not be the easiest life, but I'm my own boss, and that suits me just fine."

"Yeah, but you're my boss too," muttered Tess.

"Could be worse," Sue chuckled. "Besides, I want you to learn more about the coast. It's different up at the north end of Vancouver Island."

"But Mom, I'll miss Candice and Sea Fair and—"

"Tess, enough! We're going, and that's that. Now let's get the last of this stuff stowed." Sue turned back into the wheelhouse.

Tess slid off the icebox, keeping her back to her mother. She kicked at one of the bright orange fenders that hung between the boat and the dock. It just wasn't fair. What other kid had to spend the whole summer working on a fish boat?

From along the wharf came the sound of a familiar

whistle. Tess spun around. In a cloud of dust, Candice braked and hopped off her bike. She wheeled her bike down the ramp and propped it against one of the pilings.

"Hiya, Tess!"

"Hi, Candice." Tess scrambled off the boat. "I didn't think you were going to get here in time."

"I said I would," replied Candice, her dark eyes piercing. "You excited yet?"

Tess looked down, nudging a piece of rope with her toe.

"No," she mumbled. "I told you last night. I don't want to go. I'm scared. What if something happens? And what about getting our baskets to Sea Fair?"

"Hey, slow down, silly. I told you I'd enter them. We've been working on them all year. Old Mary says you're our best weaver even if you're not Salish. I won't forget."

"Okay," said Tess. "But I'm going to miss all the rides at Sea Fair. And all the fun. What am I going to do all summer?"

"We talked about it last night," said Candice. "My auntie lives in Alert Bay. You'll be going there, and she's a good basket-maker. She'll show you more patterns. Remember to look for the white house with three orange butterflies stuck on the porch, past the totem poles, along the shore. Or just ask. Everybody knows Auntie Betty."

"I'm sure going to miss you," sighed Tess. "I won't have anyone to talk to."

Candice grinned. "Close your eyes and don't move."

She ran to her bike and untied a Coast Salish basket. Holding it gently, she put it at Tess's feet.

"Okay. Open your eyes. It's a goodbye present! So you won't forget me," Candice said, with a look of mischief in her eye. Tess lifted the lid.

"Oh, it's so cute," said Tess, bending down to look at the little furry face staring up at her. One white ear and three white paws gave the black kitten a comical look. Tess reached into the basket to pick it up. She buried her face in its fur.

Just then Sue popped out of the wheelhouse. "Hello, Candice. I'm glad you could make it in time." At the sight of the kitten, her eyebrows shot up. She looked from one girl to the other.

There was a long moment of silence before Tess opened her mouth.

"Mom, it's— it's a present from Candice, for me, for the trip. Isn't it cute?" Tess's eyes were glued to her mother's face.

"What are we going to do with a kitten? On a boat?" said Sue.

"Mom, I'll take care of it, I promise. Please?" Tess pleaded.

"His name is Maa-mou. That's Salish for cat," Candice said, smiling sweetly at Sue.

"Please, Mom?"

Sue stood there, her hands on her hips, looking back and forth between Tess and Candice. She sighed, shaking her head. "Oh, all right," she said. "But this kitten is your responsibility. I have enough to worry about without that." Sue started the engine and stepped onto the dock. "Anyway, girls, it's time to go."

Candice gave Tess a big hug. "Good luck and go see Auntie," she whispered.

"Bye, Candice, and thanks," said Tess. "I'll write to you."

Sue untied the lines and pushed out the bow as she stepped back on board. Tess held the kitten close in her arms and turned to wave. As they headed out of the harbour, she stood on the back deck, watching the figure of her best friend grow smaller and smaller. Then Sue swung the bow northward. The harbour, her home, and her friend disappeared behind the rocky headland. They were on their way.

2

Northward Bound

The morning dragged by. For a while Tess sat at the galley table, tucked into the seat just behind the captain's chair and the big wooden steering-wheel. She flipped through the pages of her book on horses, looking at the different breeds. If she hadn't had to go fishing this summer, she could have helped out at the neighbour's stable, and she might even have been able to ride once in a while.

She sighed. Only two hours on the boat and already she was bored. Two months in this little space. What was she going to do? She got up and poked through all the little cupboards under the sink, investigating the food and the snacks her mother had packed away. Some of her favourites were there—raspberry fruit leather, chocolate-covered digestives, and peanut butter creams. But she wasn't hungry.

She sat down again, and stared out the little side porthole. They were passing through a narrow channel. The endless islands seemed to press in towards them as if trying to block their way. The low clouds wrapped around the tree-tops and oozed down the rocky slopes.

Tess felt trapped by the small space of the wheel-house, and trapped by the grey world passing by. She stood up and stretched, then climbed down the three steps into her berth, her own little bunk in the bow of the boat. She opened her pack, stuffed her clothes into the drawer under her bed, and put her favourite stuffed toy, a green turtle called Franklin, on her pillow. She carefully stowed her books on the shelf with the railing that would stop them from falling if it became rough. Not 'if,' she thought with a shudder. 'When.'

There was nothing else to do. She stretched out on her bunk, hoping she would fall asleep. But she was too restless. The diesel engine rumbled loudly, and the water gurgled and splashed against the hull.

Tess climbed back up the steps into the wheelhouse. Sue had lowered the chart table, which hung from the ceiling at the top end and rested on the galley table at the bottom. She was sitting in the captain's chair, to the left of the steering-wheel of brass and wood. She rested one hand on the wheel, and looked back and forth between the chart and the everchanging view outside. The marine radio crackled softly over the drone of the engine. She glanced at Tess.

Tess tried to ignore her. She didn't feel like talking. She didn't feel like listening to a geography or a history lesson on the wonders of the coast, something her mother was alway good at delivering at times like this. She just wanted to be alone, alone in her own bedroom, where it was safe and quiet. How could she ever be alone on a fish boat?

Tess reached into the basket and lifted out Maa-mou.

He started to purr. She tried to play with him, teasing him with a piece of string. He batted at it for a little while, grabbing it first with his paws and then his mouth. But he soon grew tired and wanted to sleep. She put him back into his basket.

Finally, Sue broke the silence. "Tess, would you please put up the next chart? You could take a pencil and mark out our route as we go. It would make a good record of our summer trip."

Tess did not answer.

"Look at that, Tess, there's an old homestead. There used to be lots of them up and down the coast. See, it's still marked on the chart, with that little black square. And there's another fish farm. There's more of them here now than the last time I was up this way."

Tess glanced briefly at the chart and turned back to stare at the view. Layer upon layer of islands stretched into the coast mountains. They had left behind the arbutus trees with their warm red bark. The dark firs and the dense cedars hung low over the water.

Sue's voice cut into her thoughts. "Look, Tess, there's Indian land. There used to be a village there. See, it's marked I.R. on the chart, for Indian Reserve. I'd like you to learn how to read charts this summer. You can learn a lot of things from a chart. The speed of water through a channel, how deep a rock is below the surface, whether the shore is steep and rocky or shallow and sandy, where to get fresh water, where to anchor and—"

Tess looked up. "Where's Alert Bay?"

Sue sighed. "The charts are in the order of our trip

up the coast. It's the third or the fourth chart down," she said.

Tess groaned. "It's that far away?"

Trying not to smile, Sue replied, "We did talk about this. Remember I said it takes about twenty-four hours of motoring time to get up there, so that means at least two days for us."

Tess slowly flipped through the charts until she found Alert Bay. She stared at it for a long time, remembering the description of Auntie's house and trying to imagine what it really looked like.

"I wonder where it is," she muttered, tracing her finger along the lines of the harbour at Alert Bay.

"What did you say?" asked Sue.

"Nothing." Tess stared out the window, lost in thought. Maa-mou suddenly woke up, stretched, and jumped up on her lap. Tess sat up and gasped.

"Mom, we don't have any cat food, or litter. What are we going to do?"

Sue raised her eyebrows. "I was wondering when you were going to think of that."

"Can we buy some where we stop tonight?"

"Our first stop with a store is Alert Bay, but we won't be there until tomorrow, and that's if all goes well."

"Mom, what am I going to do?" Tess wanted to make up some excuse, but the truth was she just hadn't thought about it, until now.

Sue looked at her. "You know, Tess, one of the most important things I learned when I first bought *Henry* was that I had to figure out problems by myself. And I often had to make do with something else if I didn't have what I needed on board at the time. Now, I did say that the cat was your responsibility. I want you to figure out what you are going to do until we can get to a store."

Tess sat looking at the kitten. He reached out a paw and batted her. He was half-grown and probably didn't need milk, but milk would do. She popped him into his basket and jumped up to look in the little fridge. Milk, eggs, cheese, what would he like?

Suddenly it dawned on her. Fish! In the live hold were herring that they would use for bait when they reached the fishing grounds.

"Mom, could I feed him some herring?"

Sue thought for a moment. "Yes, I guess so. But I hope he doesn't develop a real taste for them."

Tess put a bowl of milk by the door and set Maa-mou beside it. While he busily lapped up the milk, she scooped a herring out of the hold and set that down in front of him. Maa-mou sniffed the herring. It wiggled and he jumped back, alarmed. He stuck out his paw. Then he pounced on it as it flopped out of the way. Tess laughed.

"He's smart," she called to her mother.

Tess poked her head under the galley table and found a small cardboard box. She lined it with newspaper and stuck it on the back deck, just outside the door.

"He should be all right now, at least until we get to Alert Bay," she said.

"Good," said Sue. "We're at a wide part of the channel. You can take the wheel and I'll get us some lunch. Here's where we are on the chart. Just keep in the centre of this channel and you'll be fine."

Tess perched on the edge of the captain's chair and took the wheel firmly in her hand. It was a long reach for her, but she liked the feel of the smooth wooden handles against her fingers. She had never been able to steer like her mom did sometimes, leaning back in the chair and pushing the wheel with her foot. Tess's legs were still too short, and she did not feel confident enough to steer *Henry* with just her toe.

Guiding *Henry* through the calm waters around home had always been something Tess enjoyed. She loved waving at passing boats, particularly the tugs that pulled log booms up and down the coast. Big and slow moving, the tugs were the work-horses of the ocean. A tug was one of the few boats slower than *Henry*.

Tess glanced over at the chart, remembering Sue's comment that they were nearing rapids caused by tidal currents. Her stomach tightened. She had heard stories of boats misjudging the tides, and getting caught in currents and eddies that spun them about like toys and tossed them onto rocks, and of logs sucked down by whirlpools only to shoot straight up out of the water.

"Mom, when do we go through the Dent Rapids?"

"Around three. The tide should be turning to go with us by then," said Sue, passing her a sandwich and taking the wheel.

The *Henry Bay* swung past the safety of Stuart Island at three-thirty. On their left was Sonora Island, on their right, the rocky outcroppings of Little Dent Island with Dent Island hunched behind. As the tides ebbed and flowed, four times each day, the waters swirled through this narrow passage, creating the Dent Rapids. At times, the water rushed through at twice the speed that *Henry* could go. There were only short periods, when the tides changed direction and the current slowed, that it was possible for boats to pass through.

Tess was very quiet. She tried to put thoughts of these treacherous waters out of her mind. Sue was standing at the wheel, looking ahead with the binoculars.

"We're a bit later than I had hoped. But it looks pretty smooth," she said, handing the binoculars to Tess.

Tess looked. The water was smooth, but it was also alive. It seemed to be moving in all directions at once. Water that was flat one moment would boil up suddenly from below. Whirlpools formed and disappeared. The ocean had become a raging river. Tess put down the binoculars. Her stomach hurt. Her mouth was dry, her hands wet. She wanted to go home.

Suddenly the current caught hold of *Henry*. The engine strained as the water pushed the stern sideways. The boat listed to one side, and Sue spun the wheel to steady it. And then they were racing along, faster than Tess had thought possible. Water boiled and swirled around them. Gulls soared and swooped low over the surface, feeding on small fish that were carried to the top by the turbulence.

Tess was frightened but fascinated by the constant commotion of the world around her. She could not tell whether *Henry* was being pushed or pulled. She could feel the bow dig into the water and spin loose from a whirlpool. She could hear the engine straining as the current took hold of the boat and held them back, and then racing as the current shoved them forward. And always the low rumble of water rose above the sound of the engine.

Then, as suddenly as it began, it was over. The channel widened. The roar subsided, the water slowed. *Henry* slid into Cordero Channel, steadied, and headed west. Tess looked behind at the boiling water, then ahead at the quiet channel. She felt as if they had been squeezed out of a tube of toothpaste.

"Is it over?" she asked.

"Well, that's all for now. That was about the quietest it gets," said Sue. "It's always exciting, but it can be pretty scary, too."

"Are the Greene Point Rapids the same?"

"Pretty much. The Dent Rapids seem to have more whirlpools because the water has more corners to go around. But the current might be going a little faster through the Greene Point Rapids because we'll be a bit later going through them. But it won't be worse than this," said Sue, smiling at Tess.

Tess lifted Maa-mou out of his basket. He stretched and meowed. She carried him to the door and stood holding him tightly. What if he fell in? She knew she was going to have to let him explore the boat soon. It wasn't fair to keep him inside. Maybe tonight, when they were tied up at the dock, she could let him walk around the deck. Where would they be tonight? She hadn't really thought about it until now. The trip had been a blur of words and strange names that now would have places and faces to go with them.

The Greene Point Rapids were soon behind them. Sunderland Channel stretched ahead, with Johnstone Strait beyond. The clouds settled heavily on the sharp peaks of Vancouver Island. They motored on.

By the time they tied up at the government wharf at

Port Neville, it was long past dinner time. Tess was tired and hungry. While Sue prepared a quick meal, Tess took Maa-mou out on the back deck. He crept around, sniffing at all the new things he discovered. Tess wondered what he could smell and what the smells meant to him. He couldn't know what all the gear was for—the nets and the gaffs, the winches and the fenders, the crabnet and the buckets.

She picked him up when he wandered too close to the edge of the boat. "It's a new world for you, isn't it, Maa-mou?" she said. She held him closely. "It's new for me, too. Not the boat, but where we're going. We can help each other."

She carried him into the wheelhouse. "Can Maa-mou sleep with me?"

Sue looked at her and smiled. "I don't suppose there's any point in saying no to that question."

3

Tangled

Tess woke up to the sound of the engine starting. Sue was already up and dressed. They were heading out into Johnstone Strait before Tess had finished buttoning her shirt.

She could hardly wait to reach Alert Bay, so she could find the white house where Candice's aunt lived. And she was anxious to go to the store to get cat food and litter for Maa-mou, and postcards to send to Candice. But the day dragged on interminably. They would motor around one rocky point only to see another one waiting for them. Hour after hour of slow motoring made Tess wish that *Henry* could go just a little bit faster. She traced a fine pencil line on the chart as they inched their way northward, but it seemed to take them forever to cross one chart so that she could put up the next.

The clouds covered the ragged mountaintops of Vancouver Island, lending a sense of gloom and foreboding to the seascape as the *Henry Bay* passed Hanson Island. Navigation lights began to flash through the gathering dusk. Tess watched the chart and read off the names of the places they passed. They had seen the Blinkhorn Peninsula light. Lewis Point was next.

It was not long before she spotted the series of lights that marked the deep channel between Cormorant Island and the shallow sand banks deposited by the Nimpkish River after it tumbled down the steep slopes of Vancouver Island. Tess peered through the binoculars. She could see cars crossing the bright blue bridge! Beyond the bridge, the glitter of the lights from Port McNeill lit up the dark hills. After the hours of solitude travelling up the coast, Port McNeill looked huge. On the starboard was Gordon Bluff, the southern tip of Cormorant Island and the marker of their destination.

It was almost dark as *Henry* motored into the wide arc of the bay that gave its name to the little town stretching along its shores. Lights from the homes ringing the bay sparkled in the calm water. A large fishing fleet filled the harbour. As they approached the shore, Tess tried to figure out which house was Auntie's, but she was disappointed to discover that all the houses looked alike in the fading light. In her mind the picture of the white house with three butterflies was so clear. But she knew without asking that it was too late to go ashore and look.

Next morning the sound of her mother's footsteps woke Tess. She pulled on her clothes and climbed up into the cabin. She glanced at the clock. 7:10. The smell of coffee filled her nose. She looked out. The harbour was coming to life. Fish boats were heading out for the day, and the ferry was loading for its run to Port McNeill. The town looked bigger and better in the daylight.

"Can we go to the store now?" she asked Sue.

"First things first. Breakfast. Then we'll fill the icebox with ice. By that time the store should be open."

"Can we go see where Auntie lives, too?"

"We won't have time on this stop," said Sue. "I'd like to start fishing this afternoon. We'll probably try the other side of Malcolm Island."

"But when will we be back here?" asked Tess.

"I'm not sure. Remember, I told you we would be selling the fish either at Port McNeill or Port Hardy depending on where we are fishing. The buyer and a truck will meet us at either port once a week."

"But when will we get back to Alert Bay? Candice wants me to visit her auntie." Tess could hear the whine in her voice.

"Tess, I can't say when for sure. It depends on how many fish we catch and how long the ice lasts. Alert Bay is a good place to get live herring and ice. Speaking of which, let's wash the dishes and go fill up the icebox."

They untied the mooring lines and shifted the boat over to the ice plant, a two-storey building with the dock below and the plant above. The ice-chips poured down a big hose that hung from the top level. Their little icebox filled quickly.

After Sue paid for the ice they redocked the boat at the wharf.

"Can I have my allowance today?" Tess asked.

"Hmmm..."

"Please? We won't be near a store on Saturday."

"All right. Come on, let's go," said Sue.

"I want to get some postcards to send to Candice." Tess paused, with a shocked look on her face. "When can I mail them?"

Sue looked at her. "Next port, next week."

Tess was quiet for a few moments as they walked along the road to the store. There were so many things that she hadn't thought about when they had talked about the summer on the boat, details such as the mail and the store that she took for granted as part of her life on shore. But once she was inside the store she forgot about the problem of mailing her cards. The store was filled with everything from fishing tackle to food. While Sue headed for the fresh fruits and vegetables, Tess went to look for cat food and litter.

Near tourist mementoes and tee-shirts was a rack of postcards. Tess slowly spun the rack and looked at the pictures of sunsets, fish boats, wildlife, and smiling people holding huge salmon. She chose a card showing the totems at Alert Bay and another of orca whales leaping out of the water.

When they headed back to the boat with their purchases, Tess looked longingly down the road in the direction she knew Auntie's house must be. Next time, she thought. I hope it's not too long.

The wind from the south was rising as they headed out of the harbour. Sue turned on the radio so they could hear the weather report on the continuous marine band. Tess loved to listen to the reports and hear the names of all the lighthouses and weather stations, but she always wondered who the people were that read the reports. Their voices sounded as if they came out of robot bodies. "Winds southeast 15 to 20. Gusting to 25 in the afternoon. Seas choppy. Three-foot swells. Small craft warning for Johnstone Strait and Queen Charlotte Strait."

"It would be nice to have a break in this weather," said Sue. "It makes it easier to fish if it's warmer."

Tess sat staring at the chart. Some day, she thought, I'm going to count all the islands and rocks at the entrance to Knight Inlet. There must be over a thousand. She looked up at her mom. "Where are we going now?"

Sue looked back at her. "I'm going to try Foster Island if it's not too windy out there."

Too windy, thought Tess. And three-foot swells. Her stomach lurched. She tried to think of something else. She opened a bag of cat food, poured some in a dish, and put the dish under the table for Maa-mou. He jumped out of his basket, ran over, and began to eat and purr at the same time.

"He likes it!" said Tess.

"That's good," said Sue. "It would be hard to get him something else now for a week."

Tess sat down again and stared out the window. "When are we going to get there?" she asked.

"In a couple of hours. Do you want something to do?"

"Like what?"

"Could you start tying hooks on the lines? Do you remember how to do them?" Sue asked.

"I think so," said Tess, pulling on her heavy wool sweater. She went to sit at the wheelhouse door, half in and half out. She put the big spool of fishing line on the deck and started tying the fishing line and hooks together. The nylon line was springy. It kept slipping out of the hooks. The knots tangled.

Maa-mou came out of the wheelhouse and sat at her feet.

"I'm never going to get this right," said Tess to the kitten.

Maa-mou stood up and looked around curiously. This was all new to him. He began to prowl on unsteady legs. Tess laughed at him.

"Hey, Maa-mou, I'm not the only one that needs my sea-legs," she said.

Maa-mou stuck his nose into corners, sniffing at all the new fishy smells. He sat at the edge of the live hold and peered down into the seawater that filled the inside of *Henry*'s hull. He cocked his head to one side, watching the dark shapes of the herring as they swam back and forth in the hold.

"This is too fiddly. My hands are too cold." Tess put down the line and rubbed her hands together.

Maa-mou scampered over to Tess, tempted by the dangling ends of fishing line. He stuck out his paw. Tess tried to nudge him aside with the toe of her boot.

Mau-mou pounced at the spool of fishing line.

"Maa-mou! Look out!"

The springy line coiled around his body, and the hooks caught in his fur. The more he struggled, the more tangled he became.

"Mom!" Tess shouted. "Help!"

Sue rushed out on deck. She stood at the outside wheel and looked at the kitten and her daughter. She shook her head.

"I *knew* this cat would be trouble."

"But he's my friend," said Tess angrily.

"I know. Well, don't just sit there. Hold him still and I'll try and get him loose."

Maa-mou squirmed and fought and meowed pitifully. Tess could barely hang on to him as he wriggled frantically.

"There," said Sue, pulling loose the last hook and piece of line. "Now put him in his basket. With the lid on!"

"All right, all right," said Tess, scooping up Maa-mou and stomping into the wheelhouse.

"Tess, come here," said Sue, surveying the tangle of fishing line. "Take all this in and sort it out as we go."

Tess gathered up the lines and brought them inside. She sat at the table sulking. For a little while, she tried to untangle the lines. Then she gave up and stared out the porthole at the slowly changing scenery.

It sure doesn't feel like July, she thought. It's more like winter up here. What's so great about being here that makes Mom want to come fishing all this way? So what if there's more fish up here. It's too cold. And I know the swells are going to make me sick. She could feel the boat beginning to roll.

She slumped back down at the table, scowling as she picked up the tangled lines. Then she shoved them to one side and reached into the basket for Maa-mou. She cuddled him, burying her face in his soft fur.

"Work, work, work, Maa-mou. That's all she ever does. I hate fishing and I hate fish." Tess rubbed his ears. "At least you like them."

She found her postcards and a pen.

Dear Candice,

How are you? The trip up here was long and boring except for the rapids. They were scary! Maa-mou is fine. He is getting used to the boat. He climbs around inside but I'm scared to let him loose outside. We stopped at Alert Bay but Mom wouldn't let me go to your auntie's. She said we can visit her next time, and I hope that's soon. I miss you. We are going out fishing now for a week. What fun. Ha Ha! Write me at General Delivery, Port McNeill.

Love, Tess

Tess gazed out the window for a few minutes, then she picked up the second postcard and began writing.

Dear Candice,

This is postcard #2. I ran out of room on the first one. I drew a new pattern for a basket. I will show it to your auntie. There are so many islands up here I thought I would call it the Island pattern, and use cherry bark. Make sure you enter our baskets before the deadline. What have you been doing? Whatever it is, I'm sure it's more fun than what I'm doing. It's cold and wet here.

Love, T.

4

Jigging for Seaweed

Tess picked up the red marker and drew a line through the calendar. Day nine, the ninth day of fishing. She sighed. Nine long, cold days. Each morning they rose early and left for the fishing spot that Sue had picked the night before. Each evening Sue searched the charts for the right formation of contour lines that marked the steep-sided underwater hills where the fish liked to live. Tess was never quite sure how her mother decided on any particular spot. There were so many possible places on the charts, and they all looked more or less the same to her.

It seemed to Tess that the boat never stopped rolling. Big swells pushed in from the open Pacific, around the northern end of Vancouver Island and across Queen Charlotte Strait, and made Tess sick. She was hungry and cranky, but she didn't want to eat. Out on deck she could never get warm. The air off the water was cold and damp. Often it was misty, or worse, it rained. The drizzle seemed to cut right through her. The only time she felt warm was when she was snuggled into her bunk, but the nights were short. At the first light of day, about five in the morning, Sue rose to start breakfast and get ready for fishing. Tess often went back to sleep. But she knew that eventually she had to wake up and go out on deck. She had to face the cold and the wet and the repetition that were the pattern of fishing on this northern coastline.

What made things even harder for Tess was Sue's mood. Lying in her berth, even with her quilt pulled over her head, Tess could hear her singing. While they fished, Sue hummed along with the tape deck, singing country and western tunes. She tried to cheer Tess. She told all her old jokes and riddles and puns, but Tess had heard most of them before.

Tess sighed again as she hung up the calendar. Even the first trip into Port McNeill to sell the fish had not really satisfied her. The fish had been unloaded into the tanker truck that carried them live to the Asian markets and restaurants in Vancouver. Some day, Tess thought, she would go to the city and find a restaurant in Chinatown or a shop in the market on Granville Island that had their fish in a tank. She knew, too, that her mother had given big lingcod to the Vancouver Aquarium to use in its display tanks. Perhaps she would go there to visit the fish.

Tess pulled on her woollen socks, heavy shirt, and wool sweater. Here it was almost the middle of July. Some summer, she thought, sticking her legs into her bright lime green rain pants. She shoved her feet into her gumboots and pulled on her rain jacket. On went her gloves and toque. She felt like a stuffed toy by the time she belted her life-jacket. Taking a deep breath, she headed outside.

"Hiya, honeybun," said Sue. "Ready to start?"

Tess looked at the endless pattern of swells and the low clouds draped over the distant islands. She shrugged, discouraged already.

Sue was steering the wheel out on deck, her eye on the depth sounder, which was now swung around to face outside. The depth sounder looked like a small television. Its picture was made up of bands of colours that indicated the changing contours of the ocean floor. The fish lived on the sloping sides of underwater hills or reefs. After finding a location on the chart, Sue plotted a compass course to direct her to the approximate area. She then found the exact spot with the depth sounder. The depth sounder's picture showed her the distance between the bottom of the boat and the floor of the ocean. The best fishing spots were usually between thirty and forty metres deep.

Sue slowed the engine. "Ready, Tess? I think we're on the right spot." She left the wheel and, with a little net, scooped some live herring out of the bait hold and into a bucket of water. She took three herring and one by one slipped hooks through their backs. She carefully swung her line over the side of the boat. Each line carried three hooks a few feet apart.

Sue released the brake on the winch, which was like a big fishing reel that wound the line in and out. She held the line between her fingers as it quickly disappeared into the dark water. As soon as she felt it hit the bottom, she flicked on the brake.

"Now we'll soon see how many fish there are. This should be a good spot, Tess," said Sue, turning to look at her daughter.

Tess was standing at the fishing station on the opposite side of the deck. She stared glumly at the herring swimming around in the bait bucket. She hated this part, putting the hooks into the herring. She scooped one out. It wiggled and squirmed in her hand. She shut her eyes as she put in the hook.

Sue was busy with her line, holding it between her thumb and her forefinger so she could feel what was going on far below the surface. The hooks and the bait had to be just above the rocks on the bottom so that the fish would see them. If the line dragged on the bottom, the hooks could snag on seaweed or get caught between rocks.

"Got those herring on yet?" Sue called.

"No, Mom."

"Do you need a hand?"

"No, it's okay." Tess knew she should be able to do this part herself. It was something she could do, even if she didn't like it.

Suddenly Sue turned on the winch motor and began pulling in her line. She watched the water by the side of the boat. When a dark shape appeared, she turned off the winch motor. Holding the wooden handle of the gaff, she reached over the gunwale and slipped the hooked end into the gills of the fish. She hauled the long green body of a lingcod onto the deck where it flopped about.

"Only one. Oh, well. Better luck next time." Sue picked up the pliers and grabbed hold of the fish. "Open up," she said. "We've got to get that hook out without hurting you." She dropped the fish into the live hold. It splashed on the surface then swam quickly to the bottom.

By now, Tess had her line out. She held it tightly with one hand and held onto the boat with the other, her legs stiffly braced against the rocking of the swells.

Sue quickly rebaited her line and lowered it. "Any action yet, Tess?"

"I'm not sure."

"Here. Let me feel your line." Sue reached over and took the line between her thumb and her fingers. "No. Keep jigging."

Except for the drone of the engine, it was quiet. Tess moved awkwardly. The swells kept her off balance. She couldn't tell if her line was on bottom. It just felt heavy.

"Tess, you'd better pull in your line and check it. Maybe your hooks are tangled."

"My hands hurt," said Tess.

"But we just started," said Sue. "Aren't those gloves helping?" She pulled in her line again. "Ha! Only one fish. It should be better than this. Maybe we're not quite on the reef. I'll just swing the boat around a bit."

Tess pulled in her line, and Sue swung the boat around to the other side of the reef.

"I'll try this side," Sue said, lowering her line again.

Tess slowly let out her line, and stood forlornly jigging. She shivered, letting go of the line to rub her hands together. Her new foul weather gear and boots were no comfort to her now. She stamped her feet, trying to keep warm.

When she took hold of her line again, it felt heavy.

She jigged once and decided to pull it in. She turned on the winch motor. Maybe her line was heavy because there was a big fish on it. She leaned over and looked at the point where her line disappeared into the darkness.

Suddenly a shape, long and brown, appeared out of the green depths. She turned off the winch, picked up the gaff, and leaned over the gunwale. She stood up and looked at Sue.

"Ta da!" she said, holding up a line full of seaweed.

Sue grinned. "For a moment, I really thought you had something."

"The problem is, Mom, I can't tell where the bottom is," she said. "It's harder to feel it here. Maybe the swells make it different."

"You'll get the feel of it soon," said Sue. "You won't even notice the swells after a while."

Tess shivered again. "I'm getting cold."

Sue chuckled. "Try moving a little faster."

"I'll never get used to this," grumbled Tess.

"Oh, I hope you do. I'm going to move the boat again. We're not having much luck. I'm sure you'd feel better if we were catching more. I thought this would be a good spot, but now I wonder if it's been overfished. Maybe we'll have to go farther north."

She sped up the engine and moved the boat around to another slope. "There," she said, watching the coloured lines of the depth sounder as it took on the shape of a hill. "Let's try here."

They lowered their lines again. *Henry* wallowed in the ocean swells. Even with her gloves on, the fishing line cut Tess's fingers. A breeze came up, filled with the cold dampness of the ocean. Tess couldn't stop shivering.

Sue pulled in another fish. Tess kept jigging. Sue rebaited and lowered her line, and Tess pulled in hers. On the end was one small rockfish.

"All that work for that little fish!" She scowled. "I give up," she said as she dropped the fish into the hold.

Sue looked at Tess. "There's just no getting around it, fishing is hard. And we haven't had any breaks. Not with the weather and not with the fishing spots I've picked. I know it must be really frustrating for you."

Tess stood, shoulders slumped, looking into the live hold at the few fish that slowly circled. Tears pushed into her eyes.

"Why don't you go in and get warm?" said Sue. "This has been a rough start to the season, in more ways than one. But it will get easier. I'll take a break soon and come in, too."

5

X Marks the Spot

Inside the wheelhouse, Tess peeled off her wet gloves and hung them above the little oil stove that was their heater and on which they did their cooking. She pumped water into the stainless steel kettle and put it on the stove to heat. Leaning back against the oven, she soaked up its warmth. She sighed, tucking her hands into her armpits. Maa-mou stretched and sat up. He tilted his head to one side, staring at her.

"You'd never know it was summer, Maa-mou. I'm freezing. And there's hardly any fish. It's so boring out there. But Mom never gives up."

Maa-mou jumped up onto the chart table and batted his paw at Tess. "You silly, you want all my attention." Tess scratched him behind the ears. Maa-mou purred and rubbed up against Tess's hand. Then he lay down on the chart table, stretching out to his full length.

"I think you've grown," said Tess. She tickled his tummy.

Maa-mou rolled over and began to knead the chart table with his claws.

"Maa-mou! Stop that!"

Maa-mou dug in his claws.

"Come on!"

Tess grabbed him. As she picked him up, his claws hooked into the chart. There was a ripping sound.

"Oh, no. Now we're in for it."

Tess stood clutching the kitten, looking at the long torn strips of the chart. She glanced outside. Sue had not noticed what had happened. She was still busy fishing.

"Good thing, for once," muttered Tess as she stuffed Maa-mou into his basket and slammed on the lid. "Now what am I going to do?"

Her eyes darted around the wheelhouse. What should I do? she thought. I've got to mend it. We need the chart to navigate by. Mom will be mad. I could put some tape on it. But where is the tape? She looked through the junk drawer but couldn't find it. Think. She had used it for something. Where was it? Then she remembered. She had been cutting out pictures of horses and taping them into her scrapbook. *Always put things back when you're finished with them,* she could hear Sue saying.

She sorted through her pile of books. The tape had to be here somewhere. There it was, stuffed between the pages of her scrapbook. She grabbed it.

"Maybe this will work," she said, bending intently over the chart. She smoothed two strips of tape in the shape of an X. "There. That's almost okay."

Then Tess bent lower, and peered at the mended spot. The number 30 and the letter R below it were enclosed in a dotted circular line. Around that was another circular line. It was the same type of mark on the chart that her mother was always looking for, the contours that indicated an underwater pinnacle. Her face lit up.

"Hey, look at this, Maa-mou. It's the right depth. Thirty metres with steep sides. Maybe Mom doesn't know about this spot. Maybe this one is better than where we are now. We should try it!"

Maa-mou poked his head out of the basket and meowed.

"Mom!" Tess called excitedly.

"Hmmm?" came the vague response.

"I want to show you something."

Hearing the eagerness in Tess's voice, Sue stuck her head through the door.

"Mom, you need to come in here," said Tess.

Sue turned back to pull in her line. She pushed open the bottom half of the Dutch door and came into the wheelhouse. She looked at the chart and back to Tess.

"Well, we had a little accident," said Tess.

"Let me guess who's to blame," Sue said. The hint of a smile tugged at the corners of her mouth.

"But look! X marks the spot!" Tess pointed to the taped spot on the chart.

"Well now, that looks interesting," said Sue, taking a closer look.

"Can we try it?"

"Why not? It's close to here. Let's!"

Sue climbed into the captain's chair and took a compass reading for their destination. She sped up the throttle and swung *Henry* towards the new spot. Tess sat on the bench seat, holding Maa-mou and staring at the spot on the chart.

"Oh, I hope I'm right," she whispered to the kitten. "I hope this is a good spot. I know I haven't caught very many fish yet. If we could find a good spot for Mom, that would make up for it."

Sue kept glancing between the chart, the compass, and the changing seascape. As they closed in on the area indicated on the chart, she used the points of two islands to line up their approximate position.

"Tess, will you turn the depth sounder in to face us?" she asked.

The depth sounder was mounted by the door so that Sue could watch it from both the inside and the outside wheels. Tess turned it towards the inside wheel.

The flat rust-coloured lines at the bottom of the screen began to rise. The shape of the slope appeared and filled half of the blue screen with red. As the water beneath *Henry*'s hull got shallower, the pattern of red on the screen showed more and more of the reef. Sue cut the throttle and checked the depth again on the chart.

"We're getting close," she said, heading outside to take the controls. She spun the depth sounder to face outside again.

Tess was right behind her. Sue scanned the depth sounder's screen, and slowly brought *Henry* into position over the reef.

"See, Tess," said Sue, pointing to the red markings, "there's the edge of the reef. We're on it."

For the first time Tess was in place, ready with her line baited, when Sue gave her the nod to let out her line.

"On its way!" Tess stared at the line, concentrating on how it felt as it disappeared into the dark water. She felt it go slack.

"I'm on bottom!" she said, turning the winch. She started to jig, lifting her line once and letting it drop. As she lifted it again she felt a hard tug. "Got something!"

"Good! That was quick. Bring it in," said Sue, continuing to jig. Something tugged at her line. "I've got something, too."

Tess turned on the winch and pulled in her line. She leaned over the gunwale and watched as the shadowy shapes of two fish appeared out of the green darkness. She looked closer. She could see their large heads and thin, mottled bodies.

"Two lings!" she called.

"Great," said Sue, busy with her own line. "Now let's see," she said, dropping her fish on deck. "One big one. Well, that's a start." She unhooked the fish and tossed it into the live hold. "In you go."

Sue turned to help Tess unhook her two fish. As soon as the hooks were empty, Tess rebaited and lowered her line. "Come and get it, fishy," she said with a grin.

On deck it was quiet for a few moments except for the whirr of the winches and the squeak of the pullies as the lines ran out again. Then the lines went slack. At almost the same moment, Tess and Sue turned off the winches and began to jig.

Suddenly both lines went taut. Tess and Sue hauled them in. Again they had lings, but this time there were two fish on each line.

"Tess, can you get those in by yourself?" asked Sue,

grabbing the gaff. "I've got my hands full with these." She reached over and hauled in a big ling. It flopped around on deck while she reached over and pulled in the smaller one.

Tess looked over at her mother. She picked up the gaff and carefully leaned over the side of the boat. The fish darted away from the gaff. She waited. As the fish swam towards her she slipped the gaff into its gills and hauled it on deck.

"I did it!" Tess yelled, quickly pulling in the second fish.

As they kept working, the waves and the wind slowly pushed the boat over the reef. As the boat drifted, the depth changed and so did the catch. Tess and Sue began to pull in yelloweye rockfish. Nicknamed red snappers, they were the most colourful of the cod. Their bright orange-red bodies with large dorsal spines made them easy to spot as they approached the boat. Later Tess and Sue pulled in some china, copper, and tiger rockfish. They were smaller and easier to handle.

Sue shifted the boat around again, repositioning it onto the reef. Tess was working hard. Her cheeks were rosy. Maa-mou came out on deck and watched the fish as they flopped about in the hold.

"Great spot!" said Sue.

"Maa-mou helped me find it!"

"Makes up for ripping the chart, I guess," said Sue with a slow smile.

Just then the sun broke through the clouds. To the west, patches of blue sky appeared. Sue put down her line and stretched.

"Looks like that high pressure ridge has finally made it," she said, looking up at the sky. "Time to peel off a layer."

She stripped off her rubber jacket and hung it inside the wheelhouse. Tess put down her line. Her arms felt tired from pulling and lifting so many fish. She stood looking out across the water at the distant islands and mountains. The sombre grey of the waves slowly gave way to blues and greens. Sparkles of sunlight reflected off the ripples. The clouds gathered into round puffy shapes, leaving more and more of the sky blue. The air grew warmer.

Tess grinned and pulled off her jacket. She put her gloves back on, took a deep breath, and headed back to her station.

"This is more fun, Mom," said Tess, as she scooped out another herring.

"That's one of the things I like about this life," said Sue. "You never know what's going to happen next!"

6
Flash Visits

The *Henry Bay* was headed for Port McNeill with another load of fish. The end of week two, thought Tess. Maybe this time there would be a letter from Candice. Tess had two more postcards to mail.

Tess was feeling a lot better this time as they headed into the harbour. Somehow, during the past week, life on the boat had changed. Although the days were long and hard and often dull, the routine of fishing was beginning to make more sense. After she had located the best fishing spot so far, she felt more a part of what was going on with the boat and the trip.

Each night after dinner Sue would lower the chart table. Tess would sit with her, looking at all the possible fishing spots. Until now the charts hadn't really made sense to her. Now when she checked off the places and the ports, she understood how to relate the information to the work she and her mother were doing. Together they would discuss and pick their destinations for the next day.

Even her stomach had settled down. Her appetite returned to normal. And, to top things off, the weather had continued to improve. A high pressure ridge had settled onto the coast, bringing clear skies and westerly winds.

They tied up at the wharf. The truck was there, waiting for them. Sue went quickly to work, scooping the fish into bins for sorting and carrying to the truck. Tess sat on the icebox, counting the fish and recording the numbers on the tally-sheet.

As soon as the last fish was counted, Tess said, "Mom, can we go to the post office now?"

Sue laughed. "What about a shower first?"

Tess groaned. But she had to admit the thought of standing under hot fresh water appealed to her.

"All right," she said. "But then to the post office right after."

Sue gathered up the bundle of laundry and a change of clothes, and they headed for the showers. Although Sue was a fanatic about keeping *Henry* clean, it was impossible not to smell fishy after a week at sea. Salt spray seeped into everything.

The steamy soapy water washed away the dirt and the salt and the soreness in her muscles. As Tess dried her hair, Sue loaded up the washing machine with their dirty clothes.

"Let's go!" said Tess.

Her excitement grew as they headed up the road to the post office. She walked right up to the counter. To her surprise, the woman recognized her and handed her a packet of mail. She looked quickly through the bundle. Two magazines, one for her and one for Mom, and a couple of bills for Mom. Nothing more for her. Tess's face fell.

"It does take a while for the mail to get up here," said Sue. "Maybe next time. Don't forget to mail your cards to Candice."

Tess was quiet as they did their shopping. What was Candice doing? Who was she playing with now that she wasn't there? The water here was too cold for swimming, but it would be warm enough now at home. Candice would probably be spending her days at the beach. It was getting close to Sea Fair, though. What if Candice forgot to take their baskets? Tess had spent so many hours working on hers, and Mary had told her it was good, especially good, considering Tess wasn't even Salish. Mary loved to tease her. A great wave of homesickness welled up in Tess. She blinked back tears.

"I've been thinking," said Sue the next morning, "that we should head up towards Port Hardy and try fishing some of the spots up there."

Not farther north, thought Tess. Just when I'm getting used to things around here.

"But what about stopping to see Auntie?" asked Tess.

"Tess, that will have to wait until we come back down to Alert Bay for herring. We've still got enough for one or two weeks out. I'd like to see if the fishing is better farther north. There are fewer people fishing in that area."

Tess sighed. Sometimes she wished her mother was more like other mothers. Mothers who worked in buildings, who stayed on land, who came home every afternoon.

"What are you thinking about?" asked Sue.

Tess could feel her mother's eyes on her. What could she say that wouldn't hurt her feelings?

"I don't know." She fiddled with her spoon, then looked up at her mother. "It's— it's just that all we do is fish and work. I haven't been to see Auntie. I miss Candice. There's nobody to play with and nowhere to play. And now we're going even farther away."

Sue was quiet for a moment. "Yes, I know you miss Candice. But where we are going is not that much farther north. And it's beautiful there, more wild and rugged. We might even see dolphins. I tell you what. Let's go up for a week and try it. If the fishing is a lot better, we'll stay longer. If the fishing is about the same as here, we'll come back and fish around here. How does that sound?"

Tess wasn't sure how that sounded. More wild and rugged she could happily do without. But better fishing and dolphins would be all right. She figured she could try it for a week. She nodded.

"That's my girl," said Sue, giving her a hug. "Now let's get going."

Soon they were headed northwest again, past the Pulteney Point Lighthouse on the starboard as they left Malcolm Island behind. The expanse of Queen Charlotte Strait opened up in front of them.

The seascape began to change. Low rocky islands took shape, craggy and dark and rugged. The trees were twisted and bent by endless gales and winter storms that pushed in off the Pacific Ocean. Ancient cedars, silvered grey by rain and sun, stood guard over younger trees that pushed up to reach the light. They look as if they have been here forever, thought Tess.

Two hours dragged by. Tess could feel herself begin to fret. She couldn't concentrate on her book. She kept looking out the porthole. Her mother was right, it was more rugged. But to Tess it looked menacing.

They were passing through a channel between two large islands. The slow swells pounded the rocky shores, sending spray high into the air. Ahead to the left, Tess could see the gleaming white buildings of a light station clinging to a rocky point. What an awful place to live, she thought, glancing at the chart to see where they were.

Suddenly their radiophone crackled loudly.

"*Henry Bay, Henry Bay*, this is Scarlett Point Light Station. Can you read me? *Henry Bay*."

Tess looked questioningly at Sue as she reached for the microphone. "Scarlett Point. This is *Henry Bay*. Is that you, Anne?"

"Yes, it's me. We got transferred here three months ago. You finally back up north again?"

"Yes, I'm back. And Tess is with me."

"Well, I've got the kettle on so you'd better come in for tea."

"Sounds good. We'll head in." Sue hung up the radiophone. Tess looked at her quizzically. "That was Anne. Remember, I've told you about them. Anne and Leslie have been lightkeepers for years. I used to stop in and visit them at their other light. They're great characters, and they know a great deal about the coast. I think you'll like them."

Tess was puzzled. "How did she know it was you?"

"*Henry* is easy to recognize once you know her. There are not many of these old live hold boats left on the coast. And she's famous for her dark green hull."

Sue spun the wheel and headed towards a narrow opening in the steep, rocky shore of the point. It led into a little bay and a long lagoon, the only bit of sheltered water for the lighthouse. A floating wharf, anchored to the rock walls with cables, was connected to a boardwalk that clung to the shore.

As *Henry* pulled into the wharf, Tess watched a woman walk briskly down the wooden path towards the bay. She wore a heavy plaid mackinaw. Big black rubber boots covered her feet and a good portion of her legs. As she strode towards them along the floating boardwalk, Tess could see her round, smiling face framed with short brown hair. As she came closer to the boat, Tess was surprised to see that she was small and compact. Tess had imagined that a person would have to be big to look after and run a lighthouse.

"It sure is good to see you again," said Anne, grabbing hold of the bowline and lashing it to the dock. "I hope Leslie gets back in time to see you. She decided to go fishing this morning. Come on up."

They followed the boardwalk that led through the salal bushes and scruffy bent trees to the clearing on the point. Two small houses, the light tower and a shed, all painted white with red trim, filled the clearing. A small vegetable garden, surrounded by a high picket fence, was off to one side.

They went into the first house. Its warmth was welcome after the cold wind outside. Tess stood, trying to take in everything that she saw. She had never seen a room quite like it. Old photographs and paintings of boats, square-rigged sailing ships, coastal freighters, and tugs covered the walls. Tess knew enough about boats to know that the pictures were of the early ships that had travelled up and down the coast.

Beside the comfortable old sofa was a huge antique brass bell. Propped in one corner of the room was an ancient anchor, and, in another, part of an old steering-wheel. Piled in a twisted piece of grey driftwood were glass fishing floats in shades of aqua, green, and bronze.

"This looks just like your other place!" said Sue.

"Well, all the lighthouses are pretty similar," said Anne with a laugh. "Same floor plan, we just add all this other stuff! Milk in your tea?"

Tess was drawn to an old oil painting of a shipwreck. The ship was lying on its side, part of its hull open and exposed to the waves. Tess looked at it for several moments, imagining the force of a sea that could tear apart a ship. She thought of the rocks, and the waves pounding on them. A shiver ran down her spine.

"Look at this, Mom. What happened?" she said, looking at Anne and then back at the picture.

"That was the wreck of the S.S. *Selkirk* in 1929," Anne said.

"Where did it happen?" asked Tess, thinking of *Henry* tied at the dock. Could this ever happen to them?

"Oh, right out here," said Anne. "The keeper and his sons went out in the storm in a little rowboat and rescued the *Selkirk*'s crew. After the storm blew itself out, they rowed them to Port Hardy, the nearest town. That was a twelve-hour trip, one way. Then they rowed home to the lighthouse. Have a cookie," she said, passing a plate of gingersnaps to Tess.

"It sure must have been hard!" said Tess.

"Those were the days!" said Anne. "No phones, no electricity, no fresh food except what they could grow or catch. The rain was their water supply. They were often left for months at a time. And the only way off the island was by rowboat."

"It's not quite so bad now!" said Sue with a chuckle.

"Oh, no," said Anne. "Sometimes it's hard. But nothing like it was. Now we have motorboats, and the mail and fresh food come in once a month on the supply ship. We have radiophones and electricity, and even television!"

"But do you still get lonely?" asked Tess, glancing out the window at the expanse of water, the dark islands, and the distant wall of the coastal mountains.

"Oh, sometimes, but there's lots to do to keep all the equipment working, and we phone in the weather report every three hours for the marine radio. We also work with the Coast Guard for distress calls. We're not really supposed to do search and rescue, but sometimes we find ourselves right in the middle of things. Storms come up and boats get into trouble. Happens about once a year."

Tess chewed her cookie. *Storms come up and boats get into trouble.* We've had lots of swells, and I'm getting used to them. But what if a storm comes up? She looked out the window. It was summer now. This was not the season for storms. She hoped. Then something caught her eye.

She pointed to a large brass bell that sat on a small patch of grass in the yard. "What's that for?" she asked.

"That's the old bell for the fog signal," said Anne. "It weighs half a tonne. A weighted rope turned the gears that slammed the nine-kilogram hammer. It had to be operated by hand and wound up every three hours. Sometimes in bad weather the keepers didn't get any sleep for days. They stopped using them about forty years ago."

"What do you use now?"

"Come on. I'll show you," said Anne. "Let's take a tour."

They went out of the house and walked towards the light tower. The wind could be heard over the low rumble of the swells beating against the rocks below them. Listening to it moan in the low trees, Tess thought that the wind sounded like it had blown forever across the open seas, searching for some small island to wrap its arms around. Be still, be still, she thought as she followed Sue and Anne.

They stood at the top of the bluffs, looking north across Gordon Channel to the rocky outcroppings of the Walker islands. Behind them, more islands blended gradually into the ridges, valleys, and distant snow-capped peaks of the coastal mountains. Tess thought that every shade of blue and grey and mauve and green must somehow be here on the coast. It was rugged, but Tess had to admit it was beautiful.

"What a view!" Sue exclaimed.

"Yes, I never get tired of it," said Anne. "You know, it's funny. It can seem empty, with no sign of life, when I first look out. Then I stand here a while and just look, and before you know it, I start seeing all kinds of things. We sometimes see whales from here, and dolphins. And in the summer, the cruise ships go by. Look," she said, pointing to her right, "there's a group of kayakers. We've seen more kayakers this summer then ever before."

Tess looked where Anne was pointing. At first she couldn't see anything. Then she saw a flash of sunlight reflected off a wet paddle. Splashes of bright orange and yellow, sleek and low in the water, appeared and disappeared in the rolling swells.

"They sure are small. Could they see the light from where they are?" asked Tess.

"Oh, yes, this light can be seen for thirty kilometres. It flashes every five seconds. Each lighthouse flashes with a different characteristic—that's the length and frequency of each flash—so that in the dark, ships know which lighthouse they're near. There is also a backup light that turns on automatically if anything happens to the main light. It's the same with the fog horn, and it has a backup, too. Everything is run by electricity from the generator in that building over there."

"Well, Anne, it's been great," said Sue, "but we better get going. Time to find some fish."

They all walked down to the dock. Tess untied the sternline while Sue stepped on board and started the engine. Then Tess untied the bowline and joined her mother on the back deck.

"Okay. We're off!" said Sue. "Thanks again, Anne. Say hello to Leslie. We'll try and stop in again before we head south." She turned to Tess. "Now, I want you to steer *Henry* out."

"But Mom!"

"No buts! This is a good spot to practise. Not many places around here are as sheltered as this one. It takes lots of practice to learn how to steer, so we'll use every chance we get."

Tess stood at the outside controls. She hesitated, glancing first at the wheel, then at the water gurgling around the hull of the boat. She looked towards the entrance to the bay at the waves pushing through the channel, and turned to Sue.

"Okay," said Sue. "Put it in gear and push up on the throttle. Remember that the red lever is for the fuel and the black is for the gears. The tidal current pushing into the lagoon will push the boat in. You'll have to give her more throttle. Now turn the wheel. Harder!"

Tess spun the wheel, but not hard enough. The current caught the bow of the boat and pushed it back into the dock. Maa-mou stuck his head out the door. Anne stood watching.

"It's not working," wailed Tess, wildly spinning the wheel first one way and then the other. She could feel the boat bump again, the fenders squeaking as they rubbed the edge of the dock. She swallowed hard. It was bad enough having Mom right there, but worse with Anne watching her make mistakes. Her cheeks reddened.

"Now what?" she asked, looking angrily at Sue.

"Try again," said Sue calmly. "You need more power. Turn hard to the right, the starboard. Harder. Give it more power. You've got to get the bow around. Now it's coming. Good. You need to be going fast enough to be able to steer, and you need even more speed with a current. Good, you've got it."

The boat swung out from the dock and into the bay. Tess headed straight out. She gripped the wheel and didn't look back. She was vaguely aware of Anne's voice over the rumble of the engine.

"Good work, Tess. Come and visit again," called Anne.

Sue turned and waved. "Thanks. See you soon." She came and stood beside Tess.

"Now, that wasn't so bad, was it?" she asked.

Tess eased her grip on the wheel. She braced her legs as they headed out of the sheltered bay into the swells.

"I guess not," she said, reaching down to scratch Maa-mou's ears. It didn't seem so bad now that it was over.

"As soon as we round the point," said Sue, "you can take the inside wheel." She went forward and pulled in the fenders. Tess went inside and climbed into the captain's chair. She kept thinking about steering the boat. When Sue came in, Tess turned to her.

"Mom, when there's a tidal current or the wind is blowing, how do you know how hard to turn the wheel? Or how much power to give her?"

"Well, it takes lots of practice," said Sue. "We'll do more dockings so that you can get used to it in different conditions. I don't tell many people this, but when I first got *Henry*, I used to go down to the harbour at night and practise docking. In and out for hours when no one was around. I wanted to be able to dock her perfectly before I took her out."

Sue lowered the chart table and plotted their compass course to the fishing grounds. Tess sat at the wheel, thinking about what she had just said. She had never thought of her mother having to learn all the things that she knew and did so well on the boat. Somehow it seemed to Tess that she had always known what to do.

It was comforting to think of her mother having to learn things, too.

"Look, Tess, here's how you read the lighthouse on the chart. See this little purple mark that looks like an exclamation point? These numbers beside it give the number of flashes per minute and the greatest distance the light can be seen."

Tess did not answer. She sat staring ahead, hands on the wheel, lost in thought. They had gone by Alert Bay and they could have stopped at Auntie's. But Mom had said no each time. Yet here they were stopping to visit Anne, just like that. It wasn't fair.

"Tess, did you hear anything I just said?" asked Sue.

"What?" said Tess, turning to look at the chart. There was a long pause.

"Do you mean pardon?" Sue asked.

Tess looked at her blankly, then stared out the window. Finally she said, "Mom, I don't get it. How come we stopped at the lighthouse but you wouldn't stop at Auntie's?"

"Hmmm." Sue looked thoughtfully at Tess.

"There are some things that *I* would like to do, you know," said Tess.

"Well, you have a point," Sue admitted, somewhat reluctantly. "I'm so used to being captain, and doing things my way all the time. We were passing right by the lighthouse. And I hadn't seen Anne for such a long time."

"But we were in Alert Bay, too."

"Yes, you're right." Sue looked at Tess. "I've been anxious about getting a good catch and not sure how much extra work it would be having you with me this summer. I guess I've been going at it a bit hard." She was quiet for a moment. "I'm sorry, Tess. I'll try to take time out for fun activities. You're doing well steering. I can take the wheel now if there's something else you want to do."

"Okay," said Tess. "I'd like to write a letter to Candice."

Tess climbed down from the wheel and dug out the box of paper and pencil crayons that was tucked in the bookshelf. She squeezed into the little space at the galley table beside the chart. She chewed the end of her pencil and frowned. Then she began.

Dear Candice,

I decided to write you a letter because I have too much to say for a postcard. Besides, a letter I can put in an envelope so Mom can't read it. I'm still pretty mad at her because we haven't gone back to Alert Bay yet. I thought we would go there every week, but we'll only go there once in a while to get herring and ice. Instead, we are going even farther away, up north past Port Hardy. Just when I was getting used to it around here! It's not fair. Mom is pretty bossy. I call her Captain. Most of the time she doesn't hear me, but when she does it sometimes makes her mad. She makes me mad, too, though. All she thinks about is fishing. Sometimes it's okay, if we are catching fish, but most of the time it's really hard and boring.

How is your summer? Maa-mou likes the boat and climbs all around outside now. Sometimes I get scared that he will fall overboard. He climbed up the mast the

*other day but Mom made me get him down. No cat
rescues, she said. If he falls in, that's it. But I don't
believe her.*

"Tess. Look!"

Tess jumped up and stood at the window beside her
mother. A dolphin leapt through the bow wave. Tess
leaned out the window. Another dolphin was riding the
crest of the wave beside the boat. A third criss-crossed
the boat's stern.

"Why are they so close?" she asked.

"I don't know. They seem to come to the sound of
the engine and then like to play in the boat's wake."

For ten minutes the three dolphins stayed close to
the boat, leaping out of the waves and darting back and
forth in front of the bow. Tess could hear their high-
pitched whistles of pleasure as they played. Then, just
as quickly as they had appeared, they were gone.

"I always feel blessed when I see dolphins," said Sue.
"Somehow they make me feel safe. I guess it's because
there are so many stories of dolphins helping people in
need."

"They're so beautiful," said Tess. "I'm going to tell
Candice." She returned to her letter.

*... We just saw three dolphins really close to the boat.
They played in the waves. We saw orcas once, too, but
they were far away. Mom said that there are lots of pods
around here but we haven't seen them yet. We see lots
of freighters on their way to the east and sometimes we
see cruise ships going to Alaska. They are really big. I
wouldn't want to get in their way!*

Did you get our baskets entered on time? Please write soon. We will be back in Port McNeill in a week, I hope, unless fishing is really good and Mom decides we will stay up north. Even after we talk about it and she asks me what I want to do, we always end up doing it her way.

Lots of love and a meow,
Tess and Maa-mou

7

Small Craft Warning

Two more days and then we can go in to Port Hardy, Tess thought, checking the days on her calendar. July 20th. That means Sea Fair weekend is coming up. Maybe I'll win a prize for my basket. We've been gone three weeks, three weeks of fishing. The summer is almost half over! Only five more weeks to go, then we can go home.

Tess zipped up her life-jacket and headed out on deck. She stood beside Sue, watching the depth sounder. They were working their way along the string of reefs at the south end of the Pine Island Light Station. There was no place to land at that lighthouse. The rock on which it sat resembled a turtle, silent and alone, looking out towards the Pacific. To the south, Tess could see the string of rocks that made up the Buckle islands. Topped with old gnarled trees, twisted and bent over by the prevailing winds, the Buckles were home to a large colony of sea lions.

As she stood on deck waiting to start fishing, Tess thought of the early European explorers who had travelled through this area with no charts or lights to guide them. How strange and frightening it must have been, not knowing where they were headed. And, long before them, the Kwakiutl peoples had crossed these exposed waters in their canoes, fishing and trading and visiting other villages. They would have known their way around. Still, in comparison to their canoes, *Henry* seemed big and safe.

They had woken to a change in the weather. High clouds had covered the early morning sun as they left their anchorage at Cascade Harbour. Sue had listened to the marine band as she always did before setting out. The forecast was for light winds shifting to the southeast with the arrival of a low pressure ridge by night.

"We've been lucky with the weather so far this trip," said Sue. "I hope that low won't amount to much. If we could fish for two more days, we would have a big load for the truck."

The morning's fishing was good. Tess went in to make them lunch. She liked to be inside, out of the wind. She spread the peanut butter thickly on the bread and sliced bananas on top. Maa-mou sat watching her, licking his paws and washing his face.

Tess stuck her head out the cabin door. As the cloud cover thickened, the blues faded from the seascape. What had looked friendly was now bleak and desolate. Tess spied a line of dark grey spreading like a stain on the distant horizon. She handed a sandwich out to her mother.

"Hang on, sweetie," said Sue. "I'm coming in to check the weather again." She peeled off her gloves and came into the wheelhouse. They sat quietly eating and listening to the marine band. The storm front was moving faster than previously reported. A small craft warning was being posted for late in the day in their area.

"We're doing so well fishing on this spot, too," said Sue. "I was really hoping the wind would hold off."

They had been lucky. Tess had become used to the regularity of the swells coming in off the Pacific, but waves and wind from storms would be a different matter.

"Maybe we should go in now," she said.

"There's not much wind yet," said Sue. "I think we'll be able to fish for another hour or two."

They quickly finished their lunch and went back out on deck. The sea had turned a darker shade of grey; the clouds had completed their task of covering the blue sky. Tess did not like the look of it.

She busied herself with her line, jigging with one hand and steadying herself with the other by holding on to the stabilizing pole of the boat. She kept looking southward, watching the waves curling and breaking. Each time she looked, they seemed bigger.

"Can we go in now?" she asked, dropping a lingcod into the hold.

"Let's get a few more since we're doing so well," said Sue. "As long as I can hold *Henry* on the reef, we might as well keep at it."

"But it's getting so rough," said Tess.

"These waves aren't really that big. It's more of a chop than anything else," said Sue.

There was no use saying anything more. If Sue was going to keep fishing, she would too.

"*Henry* can take a lot more than this," said Sue, trying to reassure her.

But I can't, thought Tess. Her stomach tightened. She lowered her line again. What does it matter if we get a few more fish now? She pulled her hat down over her ears.

The wind began to gust. It was getting harder for Sue to hold the boat on the side of the reef. She would move *Henry* into position but by the time they got their lines down, the boat had been blown off course again.

The slow rolling of the swells changed. As the wind grew, it pushed up short steep waves that ran at a diagonal across the tops of the swells. *Henry* began to pitch and rock, throwing Tess off balance.

At last Sue said, "That's it, Tess. Bring in your line and we'll go in."

Finally, thought Tess, as she put away her fishing gear and headed into the wheelhouse. She hung up her foul weather clothes and warmed her hands by the stove. Through the porthole, it looked like it was going to rain.

"Where are we going to anchor?" Tess asked.

"I think we should set a course for God's Pocket. It's a sheltered spot in Christie Passage, just beyond Scarlett Point. We'll spend the night there. That way, if this storm keeps up, we'll be that much closer to Port Hardy."

"How long will it take to get there?"

"About two hours," said Sue. "We'll have to go slowly with these waves and a full load of fish. We don't want to bump the fish around too much."

Tess lifted Maa-mou onto her lap. She scratched his ears and he began to purr. She wished they had stopped fishing sooner. It would be two hours before they reached shelter and the storm was getting worse. She knew it was, even if her mother wasn't saying so. She could tell by the feel of the boat and the sound of the engine churning through the water.

All her fears and her doubts about this summer came rushing back to her. What if she got seasick? What if something really bad happened? They could hit a log or a rock; anything could happen. Or what if something happened to Mom? Then what would she do?

Tess held Maa-mou even tighter. Why did this storm have to come just when she was getting better at fishing? She had even started to enjoy parts of this trip, taking pride in what she caught, knowing it was helping her mother.

Tess looked out the window again. The rain had come. She could still make out the shape of Nigei Island and the mountains of Vancouver Island in the distance, but they were shrouded in cloud.

When she looked out the other side, she could see that they were passing close to the low rocky islets of the Buckle Group. Their dark shapes, rough and ragged, jutted out of the churning water. The waves crashed against them, sending spumes of spray over the rocks and through the few twisted trees.

For the sea lions, sunbathing was over for the day. They had abandoned the rocky ledges. Tess wondered how they felt when it was rough. Did they get scared, especially the little ones? Or did they like the waves?

"Why are you going so close to the rocks?" Tess asked her mother.

"I'm keeping them in sight because they're giving

us some protection from the waves. We'll soon have to take a compass course across Gordon Channel. It will be rougher out there because it's more exposed."

Why did they have to cross the channel? Wasn't there some closer place they could head for? Tess knew her mother must have her reasons. Sue knew these waters and she was careful. But that didn't make it any easier for Tess. Right now the ocean was too scary. And it was only going to get worse.

Henry shuddered as she ploughed her nose into the waves, sending cold spray whipping over the windows and across the deck. Grey sea, grey sky, grey islands, everything had become cold and grey.

Tess lurched over to stand at the wheel, close beside her mother. She tried to brace her legs, to steady herself against the jerking and the pitching of the boat.

"I feel sick," she groaned.

"Fresh air might help," said Sue, turning briefly to look at her. "Try standing by the door."

At the door, Tess gulped cold salty air, and glanced up at the rocky islets pounded by the churning water.

Oooh, why did we have to come? she thought, leaning her head against the door. I knew it would be like this. She cringed as the boat shuddered into another wave. Why do I have to have a mom that likes fishing and adventures? Tess wiped the tears and the salt spray from her face as she turned back inside.

"Did that help?" asked Sue.

Tess shook her head.

"We're going to head out across the channel now." Sue checked the compass as she turned the wheel. Nodding at Tess she said firmly, "We have more than an hour of rough water before we get across to shelter. I think I have a way to help make you feel better."

Tess looked up in surprise. "What?"

Sue hopped down from the chair. "Come. I want you to take the wheel."

"No, Mom, I can't. It's too rough."

"Yes, you can. I'll be right here beside you. It will keep you from feeling seasick."

Tess climbed into the chair. She gripped the wheel and looked pleadingly at her mother. "What do I do?" she wailed.

"First, look ahead! Watch the waves and keep *Henry*'s nose straight into them. When her bow falls off the waves, turn the wheel back. I'm holding her on a compass course of southeast 150 degrees."

"I don't know how—"

"Tess, you've done this before—"

"Mom, not like this! These waves are big!"

"That's true. But the main difference is keeping the boat on course. The waves push you around a bit."

Tess spun the wheel as *Henry* buried her nose into a big wave.

"Good. Keep the boat pointing straight into them."

"But, Mom, they're so big. I'm scared."

"What exactly are you afraid of?" asked Sue.

Tess didn't answer for a moment. The picture of the S.S. *Selkirk* flashed through her mind, its broken hull smashed by waves. Waves like these. In a very small voice she said, "What if we hit a rock? And sink?"

"Tess, listen to me. We have a compass and a chart. We know where we are and where we're going."

"But what if we hit something else? A log?"

"That's why we have the radar and the depth sounder on. We can use them to help us. Point a little higher into the waves."

"I keep thinking about boat wrecks. It's scary." Tess's voice trembled. She tried hard not to cry.

"Tess, I would not stay out in any condition that I thought might get dangerous. *Henry* is a strong and seaworthy old boat. She can take a lot of weather, a lot more than this. This is uncomfortable for us, and probably the fish, but not for *Henry*."

Tess peered ahead through the window with a sense of panic. The distant islands had disappeared in the rain. All she could see were the endless waves, curling and breaking as they came towards the boat. Her hands hurt from gripping the wheel. She kept staring ahead. They were alone in the middle of the ocean, all alone.

"You're doing a good job," said Sue.

Tess didn't answer. How could her mother be so calm?

"See if you can pick out a pattern in the waves. The waves usually follow a sequence. It's different depending on the area you are in, but there is usually a rhythm."

The waves all looked the same to Tess. They were too big, and too many. Wave after wave, rolling and breaking, up and down, pushing the boat to one side then the other. *Henry* rode up onto a crest, then down into a trough. On and on they went.

Then all of a sudden Tess could see it. Or maybe it was that she felt it first. She watched as the waves came steadily towards the bow of the boat. A rhythm began to form in her head. She counted the waves as they passed beneath the hull. Tess took a deep breath. "There _is_ a kind of pattern," she said. "About every sixth or seventh wave is bigger."

Sue smiled at her. "It's good to find the pattern in things. It helps to keep you prepared."

"How much longer till we get there?" asked Tess.

"We should be able to see land pretty soon."

Tess scanned the horizon. All she could see was water. The ocean, the rain, the spray all blurred together into one frightening world. And their little boat was in the middle of it, tossed about like a cork.

Then she thought she saw something. Was she just imagining it, wanting it so badly that her eyes made it up? No, there it was again. Out of the gloom she saw the faint flash of the Scarlett Point lighthouse.

"Mom! It's the light!"

Sue peered through the binoculars, then glanced at the compass. "Right on cue," she said with a grin.

"Do you think Anne can see us?" Tess asked.

"Probably. They will pick us up on the radar. I'll call to let them know we're okay and headed for God's Pocket. It will be more sheltered there than at their dock."

"How long until we get there?" asked Tess.

"Not long now." Sue picked up the microphone of the radiophone. "As soon as we pass the light and move into Christie Passage we'll be out of the big waves."

Tess turned to glance at the chart and then looked ahead again. She eased her grip on the wheel.

"It doesn't seem so rough when you're steering."

Sue smiled at her daughter. "I think it's because you can feel what the boat's going to do almost before it does it. And it gives you something else to focus on. Are you feeling better?"

Tess nodded. Slowly the boat crept past the lighthouse. The outline of Hurst Island became clearer. She could make out the shapes of trees and rocks, then they were in the lee of the island. The waves slackened, the boat steadied. Tess let out a big breath.

"Do you want to keep steering or shall I take the wheel?" asked Sue.

"I can do it," said Tess, sitting a little taller in the chair.

"I knew you could," said Sue. "Sometimes our imaginations make things worse than they really are. With practice and experience it gets easier to do new things." She hugged Tess before pulling on her jacket and heading out the door. "I'll get out the fenders. Watch for two red buoys on the starboard side that mark the entrance to the cove."

Maa-mou stood up and stretched.

"Lucky you," said Tess. "You got to sleep through the storm." But I got to steer through it, she thought. I learned how to do it. And I didn't even get sick.

Maa-mou jumped up on the back of the chair and peered over her shoulder. Tess reached up with one hand and scratched his ears.

"You know something, Maa-mou? I was really scared. That was the roughest storm I've ever been in. But now that it's over, it doesn't seem so bad. And I'll bet it's time for dinner."

Maa-mou purred in agreement.

Tess picked up the binoculars and scanned the rugged shoreline. The cedars hung down to the water's edge. She spotted the two little red buoys. But where was the bay?

"Mom," she called, "is that it?"

Sue came back into the wheelhouse. She looked out.

"That's it," she said. "Just enough room for us to tie up. There's a little dock and a floathouse. I'll take the wheel now, Captain."

Tess slid down from the chair. She was smiling. The fear of rough water that had filled her mind so many times before was gone. At least for now.

Tess found some paper and picked up her pen.

Dear Candice,

We have been fishing near the north end of Vancouver Island. Sometimes it feels like we are on the edge of the world because we can't see any more land to the west. Not like at home where we can see Vancouver Island on the other side of the strait. Up here we can see clear across the Pacific Ocean.

We just came through a bad storm. It was pretty scary but Mom made me steer and that helped. I'm glad we are now safe in a little bay called God's Pocket. Isn't that a funny name? It's not marked on the chart but that's what the people around here call it.

We were fishing near some rocky islands that had a huge colony of sea lions living on them. I think that they are the same ones that swim by our place in March when the herring are running. This must be where they spend their summer holidays. Sort of like me!

We're going to Port Hardy tomorrow. Yippee! So I

will mail this. We are half-way through the summer. It feels like we have been away forever. Sometimes when I'm fishing it feels like the day will never end and then all of a sudden the week has passed. It's funny.

Love, T.

8

Eye to Eye

The storm was still blowing the next morning. Even though it was calm in the tiny opening of God's Pocket, Tess could hear the wind moaning in the trees above the bay. The channel beyond was dusted in white-caps.

Sue had been on the radiophone the night before, making arrangements for the truck to meet them in Port Hardy a day early. Since they couldn't fish in this weather, they would cross Goletas Channel and spend the day in the harbour.

Tess knew it would be a rough ride, another two hours of churning through the waves, but as they motored out of the protection of the bay and the first of the waves slammed into *Henry*'s hull, Tess thought again of the lightkeeper and his sons rowing the rescued people across this same channel. Twelve hours in a rowboat on the stormy sea before they reached the safety of the harbour and then twelve hours before they were back again. If they could handle that, she could handle two hours in *Henry*.

As they crossed the channel, the worst of the storm

blew itself out. The clouds broke up and scattered. *Henry* headed into the big bay. Tess could see the harbour full of boats, the town behind. It seemed busy after the isolation of a week's fishing.

It was in the evening, after finishing all their town chores, that Sue said, "You know, Tess, I've been thinking about fishing this far north. There are more fish up here, but it is very exposed. I guess that's why I love it. But I think that we should fish around Port McNeill. Just in case something should happen to me, or the boat. There are more safe harbours and more people in that area."

Tess panicked. Something happen to Mom! What did she mean?

Sue saw the look on Tess's face. "Not that anything is going to happen," she said quickly. "It's just that I think it's more sheltered there. The swells are smaller and it will be easier for you on deck."

Next morning, the boat emptied of her load of fish, Sue turned northeast. Over the next couple of days, they worked their way down along the northern rim of Queen Charlotte Strait.

The good weather returned. When Tess could get out of the wind, she actually felt warm. And her mother was right: the swells at this end of the strait were smaller. The gentler, more familiar seascape made her happy.

There was always something new to see as they moved from one fishing spot to another. Tugs pulled barges filled with logs or heavy machinery. Large freighters crossed Queen Charlotte Strait on their way to Johnstone Strait, the most direct route to the southern ports. Once in a while a cruise ship, glistening white, would glide by, dwarfing everything as it passed on its way to or from Alaska.

One morning Tess and Sue were fishing along Egeria Shoals, in the north end of Blackfish Sound. The sun was warm, the sea calm. A glaucus gull swooped low overhead, its white and grey body gleaming in the sun. It let out a shrill cry and flew on.

Now Tess moved quickly and easily about the boat. Her hands and arms had grown stronger. She was able to feel her line as it hit bottom and she could usually feel a fish strike. While she fished she liked to watch the gulls soaring overhead and the water birds scooting over the surface hunting for food.

Maa-mou was happier, too. He prowled about the deck on steady legs, looking for something to do. He pounced on real or imagined flies, batted at rope ends, and climbed up and slid off the smooth red fenders. The boat had become his backyard.

"I'm glad we came back down here," said Tess. "I hope there's a letter from Candice the next time we go in."

"So do I," said Sue. "It's good to get news from home. There should be a letter by now." She paused to stretch. "You know, I'm really pleased with how well things are going. Maybe I won't have to work at the store so much this winter. We could take a holiday."

"Could we go to Mexico?" asked Tess.

"I don't know," laughed Sue. "That would be fun. But, right now, I was thinking about money. And I think that some of the profits should go to you since you've been working hard."

"What do you mean, Mom?"

"After I pay the expenses, the fuel, and the food, we could divide the money. Most of it would be for us to live on throughout the winter. But the rest we could share, some for me and some for you to buy something special."

Maa-mou perched on the rim of the live hold and gazed wistfully at the fish. Then he paced back and forth, his tail twitching.

"How much will that be?" Tess asked.

Sue grinned. "That depends on how many more fish you catch!" She thought for a moment. "It would probably be about a thousand dollars."

"All for me?" exclaimed Tess. "A thousand dollars?"

"Yes," said Sue. "But I get some say in how you spend it!"

"I know, I could get a horse!"

"On a boat?"

Maa-mou stood on his hind legs, his front paws on the rim of the small bucket of live herring bait. He peered in, eyeing the darting fish. He reached out a paw, trying to catch one. Maa-mou and the bucket tumbled over, spilling herring and water across the deck with a crash. Maa-mou grabbed a herring in his mouth.

"Maa-mou!" and "That cat!" yelled Tess and Sue together.

Tess grabbed the guilty cat, who managed to swallow most of the herring. Sue rescued the remaining fish, muttering, "When will that cat learn?"

Tess put Maa-mou on top of the wheelhouse and went back to her fishing station. The thought of all that money was a whole new aspect of fishing that she hadn't considered. "I know, I could get a T.V. for my bedroom."

Sue groaned.

"I know, Mom, how about—" Just then a flash of movement caught her eye. In the distance, a black fin broke the surface and was gone. Another surfaced behind it, then another.

"Mom, it's orcas!" Tess grabbed the binoculars and scanned the horizon. She tried to count them, but the rocking of the boat made it impossible. "I can't tell how many there are. Maybe five or six."

"I'm going to call the Orcalab. We're close enough to them that they'll want to know we've made a sighting," said Sue, reeling in her line. "Do you remember the stories I've told you about Paul?"

"Is he the scientist that lives near here?" asked Tess, putting away her line.

"Yes." Sue headed inside. She stopped by the chart. "We're here," she said, pointing to the shoals. "And this is Hanson Island. Paul has his home and lab right here." She pointed to a small bay on the southeast end of the island.

Tess studied the chart. "Why is this called Blackfish Sound?"

"Orcas are called blackfish as well as killer whales. And this is one of their favourite spots." Sue picked up the radiophone's microphone.

"Orcalab. Orcalab. This is *Henry Bay*."

A crackly voice replied, "*Henry Bay*. This is Paul at Orcalab. Come in."

"Hi, Paul. We just spotted some orcas headed south. I'm not sure how many, maybe five or six."

"There's more than that," interrupted Tess, the binoculars glued to her eyes.

"Tess is with me this summer. She thinks there are more than six."

"Thanks, Sue. We should start picking them up on the hydrophones. Since you're in the neighbourhood, why don't you stop in for a visit?"

"Thanks, Paul, we will. I'd like you and Tess to meet. We'll see you soon."

"Are we going there right now?" asked Tess.

"Sure. Our lines are in and it will be a nice break," said Sue, speeding up the throttle.

For a short while Tess kept the orcas in sight, but they changed their direction and disappeared behind Swanson Island.

Sue headed *Henry* south across Blackfish Sound and followed the north side of Hanson Island. They motored around a rocky headland and a little sandy bay opened before them. A cluster of buildings, weathered grey and almost hidden by cedars and honeysuckle vines, clung to the rocks. A flash of colour caught Tess's attention. People and kayaks were on the shore.

Sue dropped anchor and they climbed into their rowboat. As they rowed into shore, Tess saw a man on the rocks. She knew Paul was a marine biologist who had done pioneer research with orcas. But was this him? This man was dressed in cut-off jeans and an old sweatshirt. His hair, streaked with grey, sprung out from his head in all directions. His feet were bare yet he hopped about on the rocks with no apparent discomfort. And, as they got closer, Tess looked into the most piercing blue eyes she had ever seen.

He grabbed the bow of the rowboat. "Good to see you again, Sue. It's been a long time."

"And you, Paul. This is my daughter Tess," said Sue.

"Hello, Tess." Paul took her hand as she climbed out of the boat. He turned to the tall woman standing beside him. "This is Christine. She's a nature photographer. She's up visiting for a month."

"We've discovered an eagle's nest up the shore," Christine said. "We were just getting ready to go. I'm hoping to photograph it." Christine lowered her gear into a single kayak.

Paul pointed to the double kayak in front of him. "I'm taking this one. Would you like to come with us, Tess?"

"In that?" Tess shook her head. "No, I don't think so."

"I know it's not *Henry*, but it's perfectly safe," said Paul.

"I've been out in it," said Sue. "It really is more stable than it looks. Try it, Tess. I think you'll enjoy it."

Tess looked at the kayak, her mother, and then at Paul. They were both looking at her. "Well—"

"Come on," said Paul. "I'll tell you what. If you don't like it, I'll bring you back."

"Oh, okay," said Tess reluctantly.

Tess pulled the spray skirt over her life-jacket. Paul steadied the kayak as she climbed in carefully. He handed her the double-bladed paddle, eased the kayak out into the water, and climbed in.

Christine headed off first. Paul paddled closely behind. Tess gripped her paddle, afraid to use it for fear of tipping the kayak. It felt odd to be sitting below the water-line.

They were soon out of the little bay. They rounded the point and headed west along Hanson Island. They passed so close to the rocky shoreline that Tess could see beneath the surface of the water. Bright orange and purple starfish clung to the rocks, crabs scurried under seaweed, and the tentacles of green anemones swayed in the current. Tess was so fascinated that she forgot to be scared.

"We used to use kayaks and rubber rafts a lot in our research," said Paul. "We could get close to the whales in them. But now we have decided to do our research on shore so that we don't disturb them. Figured there are too many other boats around anyway. Now we have hydrophones in the water to pick up and record the sounds and the movements of the whales. They send the signal to the lab where it is recorded on tape and on graph paper."

Tess carefully dipped her paddle in the water. She stroked gently in time with Paul's strokes. The two kayaks glided quietly along the shore.

"Do you ever see orcas now when you're out kayaking?" she asked.

"Sometimes. If we're lucky!" said Paul.

"Isn't it scary?"

"Well, sometimes they come close because they are curious, but they wouldn't hurt us. Orcas know exactly where everything is. They bounce sounds off objects and wait for the echo to come back. We call it echolocation."

They turned and paddled into one of the many bays that cut into the north shore of Hanson Island. Between the numerous rocky outcroppings that filled the mouth of the bay, the water was shallow. Tess could see the bay's sandy bottom covered with long green fronds of eelgrass undulating in the current.

She heard a rustle on shore. A mink raised its head to watch them pass, then went back to eating its sea-urchin lunch. In front of them, Christine had stopped paddling. She raised her camera to her eye.

"Look," said Paul softly, pointing above them. "There's the nest. And there's one of the eagles. Watch."

At the top of an ancient cedar snag, its silvery branches gnarled and bent, was a messy collection of sticks. Perched on the edge of the nest sat a bald eagle. The white of its head contrasted sharply with its dark brown body.

They sat in the kayaks, drifting silently. Another adult eagle flew to the nest, a fish clutched in its claws. There was a flurry of excitement. The small heads of the baby fledglings popped up and down as they scrambled and fought for their share of food.

Suddenly the quiet of the bay was interrupted by a sound from behind them, beyond the ring of islets that dotted the mouth of the bay. Tess froze. If the sound was what she thought it was, she did not want to be in the kayak.

She looked around. Beyond the islets, the sunlight sparkled on the rippling water of the sound. Everything seemed calm. Maybe she had imagined it. Christine was still busy taking pictures.

Then she heard it again. There was no mistaking it this time. Tess knew what it was, but she still had to ask.

Her voice squeaked out. "What's that?"

"Well, it's your lucky day," said Paul, turning the kayak around. Christine spun her boat around and came alongside them.

"Let's go out to the mouth of the bay," she said excitedly. "We won't be in their way there, but I should be close enough to get some good pictures."

Without waiting for an answer, she was off. Paul followed right behind her. Maybe if I only pretend to paddle, Paul won't notice, Tess thought. Maybe the whales will have gone by the time we get there. But it was no use. The kayaks sliced through the water and passed the islets. The expanse of Blackfish Sound opened before them.

Tess sat without moving, gripping her paddle. She stared at the water before her. The familiar shape of a black dorsal fin broke the surface. The whooshing sound of air exploding from a blowhole reached her ears. It was a pod of orcas. And it was coming towards them.

As one whale sank below the surface of the water, another whale would rise up, the sun glistening off its white and black body. A puff of vapour rose in the still air. Then two whales surfaced together, a mother with her baby close at her side. As they sank below the surface, yet another huge body exploded out of the water, flinging spray high into the air.

Tess had seen orcas before. They passed by Lund, always far out in the strait. But now she was in the water with them, in their own element. And she was in a tiny kayak. The whales were bigger than the kayak, and they were moving quickly, much faster than the kayak could.

"It may be the same pod you saw earlier," said Paul.

Steadily and effortlessly, the huge mammals moved through the water, their bodies gleaming in the sun. Tess could smell the faint acrid scent of salty vapour as it drifted over the water.

Now it was easy to count them. There were eight in all, two small ones close beside their mothers, a bigger one with a notch in its dorsal, and three others.

Tess realized that Paul was talking to her. "The families are matriarchal. The oldest female is the head of the family and her children and her grandchildren live with her. She has the most experience and memory, so she's responsible for the pod."

"They're so big," said Tess. She couldn't stop the trembling in her voice. What if they make a mistake? What if they think that the kayaks are logs, and bump into us?

As if Paul could read her thoughts he said, "We'll just wait here and watch them pass. They're big, but they won't hurt us. They are aggressive when hunting for food, but that is salmon, not us. In their family groups, they are peaceful and co-operative. And they're on their way to somewhere else today."

The largest whale separated from the pod and moved towards the kayaks. She swam along the surface parallel to them. She stopped and raised her head out of the water to get a better look at her visitors.

"That's A-11. She's the oldest, coming to check us out. I gave her a back scratch once, when I was studying them from the rubber raft."

"How do you recognize her?" asked Tess.

"Each whale has a patch of white, called a saddle, just behind the big dorsal fin on its back. The saddle and fin are different on each whale, making them just like a human thumb-print. They help us tell them apart."

The whale was so close that Tess could see her black eye looking back at her. Tess was filled with a rush of emotions, terror and awe, yet a sudden sense of calm. She knew that, somehow, this large mammal was as curious about her as she was about it. And it would not harm her.

She glanced around. Christine had let her boat drift a short distance away. Tess could hear the camera clicking again and again. Paul sat silently behind her, watching the whale. Without a noise, the whale slipped back below the surface of the water, as if knowing not to rock the kayaks with her waves. Tess sat motionless. Where had the whale gone now?

It seemed to take forever before the orca resurfaced farther away. With a loud smack of her tail she dove again and rejoined her family as they headed southward.

Tess realized that she had been holding her breath. She gulped. "They're so beautiful," she said, her voice filled with wonder.

"Yes, they are," said Paul. His voice, too, was hushed. "I'm so glad we shared this. I don't often get this close to orcas anymore." He paused. "They are so perfectly suited to their environment. They've really figured out how to live and work together. We have a lot to learn from them."

Christine paddled towards them.

"Got a wonderful shot of you and the whale," she called.

"She must get some good pictures," said Tess.

"Yep, she's one of the best! She sells lots of pictures to wildlife magazines." Paul started to paddle again. "Got enough, Chris?"

"More than I expected! Let's head back," she replied.

Later that evening as *Henry* swung gently on her anchor rope, and Tess and Sue sat at the table finishing their dinner, Tess's face lit up.

"Mom, I have a great idea! Can I spend some of my money on a camera?"

"That's a wonderful idea," said Sue.

"I could take pictures of animals and places around here. And I could start a photo album of our trips. Chris has a telephoto lens. If I got one, I could take nature shots like she does!"

Sue smiled. "I'll help you choose one if you like."

9
Past the Totems

There it was. Finally! Right on the top of the bundle of mail the woman had just handed to her. Tess would have recognized that printing anywhere. She handed the rest of the mail to her mother and tore open the envelope.

Her eyes scanned the words. It had been hot. Candice had been swimming. She missed her. Yes, she had entered their baskets in the craft show. She was looking forward to Sea Fair this weekend. Tess checked the date on the letter. July 15th, she thought. That's almost three weeks ago.

She kept reading. One of Candice's cousins was driving up Vancouver Island and could bring her to stay with her auntie. They were coming about the end of the first week in August.

"Mom! Mom! Candice is coming!" Tess jumped up and down. "Candice is coming to stay with her auntie!"

"When?"

"The end of the first week in August. That's soon, maybe now. What's today?" Tess asked, looking around the post office for a calendar. "It's August 5th. Maybe she's there now. Can we go?"

"Not tonight, but we'll go over in the morning. We need to get more ice and herring, so that will work out well," said Sue.

Tess had no problem waking up the next morning. They slipped out of Port McNeill and motored the half-hour across to Alert Bay. The bay was calm, the light golden as it touched the tops of the fish boats at the dock. But although it was still early, it was already busy at the fish plant. At one dock, boats unloaded their catch. At the other, boats waited for ice. Sue positioned *Henry* into the back of the ice line.

One by one the boats edged up to the ice dock. Some boats had huge ice holds and took a long time to fill. Others, like *Henry*, had only small iceboxes, or had refrigerators and freezers. They only needed a small amount of ice and were quickly filled.

There was only one more boat in front of them now. Sue kept looking at her watch. Tess finished wiping out the icebox. She had finished her chores in record time. She watched impatiently as the boat in front of them untied its lines and sped up its engine.

"Our turn," Tess said, her eyes shining. She couldn't help looking along the shore, past the burial grounds and the memorial poles. Somewhere beyond them was the big white house with the three orange butterflies.

Tess picked up the bowline and stepped onto the dock. As Sue squeezed *Henry* into the tight space, Tess pulled the rope snug and tied it down. Maa-mou ran to the bow and reached out his paw. Tess ignored him. Her mind was elsewhere.

"Mom, can I go now?" she called.

"Not right now, Tess," said Sue, grabbing the big ice-hose and carrying it over to the icebox on the back deck.

"But, Mom, you said when we got ice."

"I know, I know," Sue said impatiently, as she signaled the loader to start the flow of ice-chips down the chute and into the hose. "But we've got to load the ice and get out of here. Look at all these boats still waiting behind us. I didn't think it would be this busy."

Maa-mou leaned out from the bow, trying to gauge the distance from the boat to the dock. The ice began to pour into the box.

"Can I just run down to Auntie's house to see if Candice is there? I'll come right back. Please, Mom. Can I?"

Maa-mou crouched, poised to jump to the dock. The ice continued to pour into the box.

"Tess, just wait. I've got to watch the ice and get the herring."

Maa-mou sprang from the bow. But his jump was short. With a splash he landed in the water between the boat and the dock.

"Mom!"

Tess threw herself down on her stomach and tried to grab the kitten struggling in the water below. "Mom! I can't reach him. Help!"

"Between you and that cat." With one arm still wrapped around the ice-hose, Sue reached with the other and grabbed a hand-net. She tossed it to Tess. "Maybe it was a mistake to bring you. And the cat," she muttered under her breath.

Ice began to overflow from the box. Ice-chips poured onto the deck. "Oh no!" Sue yelled up to the loader. "Stop!"

The hose emptied. Sue stood, her boots covered in a mound of ice, looking at the mess.

Tess lifted the net with its bedraggled contents onto the dock. Maa-mou leapt out of the net, bounded onto the boat, and disappeared into the wheelhouse. Tess took one look at the ice on the deck and her mother's face and turned and ran. Up the ramp and along the wharf to the road that led to Auntie's house she went, without stopping to think about what she had done.

She was out of breath both from fear and running by the time she passed the burial ground's memorial poles. She slowed down to a fast walk, checking each house she passed. There were several white houses, but none had butterflies on the porch.

Just when she was beginning to wonder if she had gone too far, Tess glimpsed a pair of long legs, a head of short black hair, and a familiar purple and white tee-shirt, and gave a yell of delight. There was no doubt in Tess's mind that this was Auntie's house, for who was on the steps of the front porch but her best friend! She ran up the path.

"Candice! You made it! I didn't know if you'd be here yet," she said breathlessly.

"Good timing! I got here early, two days ago," said Candice with a grin. She turned to the woman sitting in the chair. "This is my Auntie Betty."

Auntie Betty's face was round and wrinkled. Her long black hair, streaked with white, was pulled back and tied at the nape of her neck. She nodded to Tess, her black eyes smiling hello.

Auntie was busy. With her teeth she held the end of a strip of cedar bark. With her strong hands she was carefully pulling the strip apart into thinner pieces. More cedar bark strips were soaking in a bucket at her feet. She was splitting the bark to weave it into baskets.

"Guess what?" asked Candice.

"What?" asked Tess.

"Guess."

"I don't know. Tell me," said Tess.

Candice smiled and waited a moment. "You won second prize for your basket."

"Oh!" Tess jumped up. She wasn't quite sure what to do or say.

"They gave your basket a big red ribbon," said Candice.

"Did you win anything?" asked Tess.

"No," said Candice. "I'm not as good as you. But Auntie's going to take me to an island where she gathers bark and roots to make baskets." Candice turned to Auntie. "Can Tess come too?" she asked.

Auntie took the strip of cedar out of her mouth. "It's okay with me," she said as she began working the strip with her hands. "Candice was telling me that you make baskets too. I'll show you how the Kwakiutls do it. You might learn something different from those Salish!" Auntie chuckled.

"I'd love to go." Tess gulped, thinking of the disaster she'd left behind. "I—I don't know if Mom will let me. When are you going?"

"This afternoon. We're going to Memcwumlees,

that's where the Mamalilicula people used to live," said Auntie.

"Where?" Tess's eyes popped wide open.

"On Village Island," laughed Auntie, "not very far from here. Your mom will know."

"I better go ask Mom," said Tess. "If she says yes, we'll meet you there. Okay?"

"Sure. See you later," said Candice.

Tess hurried back to the dock. She stopped at the top of the wharf and looked down. *Henry* was all clean and redocked at the public wharf. Sue was just putting away the mop. Tess walked quickly down the ramp.

She took a deep breath. Her heart was pounding as she tried to figure out what she could say to make things better. "I'm sorry, Mom," she said quietly.

There was a long and heavy pause. "Well, so am I." Sue sighed. "I didn't mean it was a mistake to bring you. I love having you with me. It's just that sometimes I feel pressured when there's too much to do. I wasn't saying that you couldn't go to see Candice this time. I just wanted you to wait until we could go together, after we had finished with the ice and the herring."

Tess climbed on board. "I'm trying my best."

"I know you are. And maybe I expect too much. You've done well." Sue smiled. "I know how much you wanted to see Candice, and her auntie."

Tess's face lit up. "Mom, Candice is here! And her auntie's taking her to where they gather bark and they asked me to come too. Can we go, Mom, please?"

"Slow down. When? Where?"

"This afternoon, on Village Island. Auntie said you'd know where it was," said Tess.

"They must be going to the old village of Memcwumlees."

"That's it. Can we, Mom? Please?"

"But what about fishing?" asked Sue.

"I know, we can fish all morning, somewhere close, and then meet them this afternoon. Please, Mom?"

Sue looked at Tess's eager face.

"Yes," she said. "We can go."

Early that afternoon, *Henry* nosed slowly through a string of low rocky islands covered with little evergreens, and headed into a shallow, sheltered bay. A single grey totem pole, leaning to one side, stood as a memory of the once busy village of Memcwumlees. Thimbleberries all but covered the few weathered buildings that remained, some standing, some partly fallen. Sue went forward on the bow and dropped *Henry's* anchor. Sue and Tess climbed into their rowboat.

As they rowed ashore, Tess looked all around her. She had a funny feeling, as if she were being watched. It was hard to put it into words. "Mom," she said, "it feels as if the people should still be here."

"Yes," said Sue, "if you close your eyes it's easy to imagine a village here. It's a perfect spot, sheltered from the wind and the weather. But it's still open enough to see anyone approaching from a long way away. There must have been lots of fish and game all year round. No wonder people lived here for generation after generation."

Candice and Auntie were sitting in the tall grass at the top of the bank, waiting for them. The air was warm and still, and filled with the hum of bees. They made their way along the trail, past fallen totem poles and old log roof beams from the bighouses, and entered the dark forest that bordered the clearing. It was cool and very quiet.

Auntie walked up to a huge cedar tree. She pointed at the trunk. A long strip of bark had been peeled off, leaving a scar. The tree had healed with new bark growing over part of the strip.

"See, there's an old mark. See how long it is." She pointed at a shiny bare strip. "And this is a new one. We gather the bark around here in June when the sap is running and the bark comes off easily."

The forest floor was soft beneath their feet. The huge cedar trunks rose up towards the light. They walked deeper into the forest. Around them, the air was still, but far above their heads the breeze whispered in the tree-tops. A raven croaked. There was a distant answer.

Auntie stopped and pointed to several cedars. "Look at the trunks," she said. "You can see that lots of strips have been peeled off. Some strips are old ones and some are newer ones. We've been here a long time. But when we take the bark, we take only a little bit from each tree so that we don't kill it. We want the trees to keep growing. We tell each tree that we need it and we thank it for helping us."

Tess and Candice ran up to an old cedar. Tess stood on one side and Candice on the other. They leaned against the tree and stretched their arms out as far as they could. But the tree was so large that they could not touch each other's hands.

They ran back to Auntie.

"What do you do with the bark?" asked Tess.

"We split the inner bark from the outer bark. Then

we wrap up the inner bark and take it home to work on it. We used to use the outer bark to make bailers for emptying water out of our canoes, and to make boxes for storing food and blankets. In the old days, we used the inner bark for all kinds of things. We shredded it to make it soft for clothes, and we split it to weave into baskets and blankets. We made string from it, and our clothing—hats and rain mantles, skirts and vests. We even used it to make sails and harpoon lines."

"Did you use other parts of the tree?" asked Tess.

"Oh, yes, we used everything," said Auntie. "Some trees we cut down to build our bighouses and to make our canoes. We would carve lots of things, masks and spoons and paddles. And we used the roots, too, for weaving and ropes, baskets and baby boards."

"What do you use cedar for now, besides basket-making?" asked Tess.

"We still use cedar for many, many things," said Auntie. "We split the bark to decorate masks and costumes for some of our dances, and for headbands for our potlatch ceremonies. We are building cedar canoes again now, and carving masks and spoons and paddles. And we are teaching you young ones how to make the root and the bark baskets."

Candice had wandered off. Basketwork was not her favourite pastime. She knelt down beside a fallen trunk.

"Tess," she called. "Come see!"

Tess ran over and knelt beside her. A miniature forest of mushrooms grew out of the rotting wood. A snail crept through the stems. Fern fronds arched over, forming a natural frame around the scene.

"I wish I could paint that," said Candice softly.

"If I had a camera I would take a picture," Tess whispered back. Tess rested her chin on her hand. She looked at Candice, her face absorbed in watching the snail. It feels so good to be with her again, Tess thought, wishing the afternoon would go on forever.

She looked up. Sue and Auntie had walked farther along the path. She could see Sue nodding and pointing, listening carefully to Auntie. After fishing, her mother's next favourite thing was plants. Just before Sue disappeared from view, Tess nudged Candice.

"Come on," she said, jumping up. "I'll race you."

The two girls dashed through the forest. They were panting when they caught up to Auntie and Sue.

Auntie stopped and looked up into another cedar. She pointed.

"See those skinny things?" she asked.

Tess looked up. She wasn't sure where Auntie was pointing.

"Those things that look like little branches hanging off the larger ones?" she asked.

"In English, they are called withes," said Sue.

"Yes," said Auntie. "In Kwak'wala we call them taxám. We use them for baskets." She pointed to the berry basket slung over her shoulder. "Here they are. I use them for the frame of the basket because they are strong."

"Can we pick some berries now?" asked Candice.

"Always thinking about your stomach!" said Auntie with a chuckle. "Off you go."

The girls ran along the path through the cool forest and made their way back to the clearing. The branches of the bushes were laden with thimbleberries. Soon

Candice's lips were stained red with juice.

When Auntie and Sue caught up to them, Tess stopped picking berries to look more closely at the basket.

"Your berry basket is different from the Salish ones," said Tess, noticing the pattern of light and dark bark.

"Yes, we make them a different shape and we have different designs," said Auntie. She looked sharply at Tess. "I tell you what, Tess, you make a basket and next summer you bring it to show me. Okay?"

Tess looked at her mother and back to Auntie. She grinned.

"Next summer for sure. As soon as we're back! Now can we go swimming?"

Sue nodded. "I'll go out to *Henry* and get some food. Let's have a picnic supper on the beach."

The two girls ran down the bank. Their clothes were off by the time they hit the shore. The tide was high. The beach was covered deeply with broken clamshells, built up over many years of habitation. The water, a deep blue-green, glistened in the late afternoon sun.

The girls dashed in, shrieking with the shock of the cold water against their warm bodies. Tess dove under and surfaced, rolling over on her back. She lay suspended between ocean and sky, wrapped in blue. She closed her eyes.

This was summer, she thought. Candice and swimming and being stuffed with berries. Summer can happen here, too.

10
Mayday!

The days were getting shorter. The sun was lower in the sky and cast longer shadows and shafts of light through the trees of the islands. Each night the evening began a little earlier, covering the deck with dew, making it slippery and wet in the morning. And when Tess got up the air was still cool and moist. It took longer for the sun to warm it.

The leaves on the maple trees were tinged with bronze. The colours of the distant mountains seemed to soften. The air smelled different as it blew across the water carrying with it the scent of drying leaves and sunburnt needles.

Browned from hours spent on deck, Tess now moved nimbly about the boat. Life had fallen into place, and each day offered something new, even if only in small ways. The ocean was sometimes gentle and sometimes fierce, but it no longer frightened her.

Tess still couldn't figure out how Sue could keep fishing for hours at a time. But she had worked out a schedule of activities for her day. She would fish for two hours in the morning. Then she would take a break and go inside.

On the last stop at Alert Bay, Tess and Sue had gone to the museum and the library. They had spent the morning looking at the collection of masks, baskets, and carvings of the Kwakiutl nation, and Tess had borrowed some books from the library. She had found a book on the early settlements of the coast. It told about the homesteads and the floating camps, the numerous canneries that processed the fish in the days before ice and refrigeration, the lighthouses and their construction, and the markers that made the coast safer for mariners. She would curl up with the book and read until lunch.

Tess liked having her own schedule for the day. After their lunch break, she would usually fish for another two hours and then take another break. Knowing that she only had to fish for two hours at a stretch made it easier. And if the fishing was good, she would keep on working, caught up in the excitement.

Sue let her take the wheel more often, and whenever it wasn't too crowded or busy at a wharf, she insisted that Tess try docking. It was hard. Feeling self-conscious, Tess understood now why her mother had chosen to practise at night. But twice she had been able to get *Henry* close enough that Sue could jump to the dock with a bowline.

Tess's favourite time of day was the evening. From the moment that Sue put down her line, stretched and said, "That's it," Tess looked forward to all the routines and the rituals of the evening. It was her job to swab the deck as Sue peeled off her wet gear and went inside to steer to their anchorage. Tess would dip a bucket into the live hold and dump it onto the deck. Then she would scrub the deck with a long-handled round brush, sloshing the water out of the scuppers. She would put all the buckets, gaffs, and nets away. Maa-mou often came out to help her, dodging the brush as he darted about playfully.

Tess loved the stillness that settled around them once *Henry* was anchored in a calm little bay. Often the only sounds were those of the water gurgling around the hull, the shore birds singing their last songs of the day, and the distant cry of gulls.

The lights of the cabin made it feel warm and snug as the darkness gathered outside. They often had fish for dinner, but Tess didn't mind. She was always hungry, and her mother knew many different ways to cook fish.

It was hard to believe that the summer was almost over. When they had headed northwest at the end of June, the two months had seemed to stretched forever in front of her. Now there were only two weeks left before they would head southeast to Lund, back to land, home, and school. It would be good to see her friends again and go up to the farm to see the horses. But Tess knew now she would miss this life on the boat. She knew she would never be able to explain it to her friends, not even Candice. It was so different from anything that they did. There was something magical about living on a boat for this long a time. *Henry* had become her home, safe and secure, in this constantly changing seascape through which they moved. And there was something magical about this part of the coast, with its rugged rocks, its turbulent currents, its still waters, and its sheltered bays.

It was a land of drama and contrast.

Maa-mou rubbed against Tess's leg, interrupting her thoughts. With one hand on her line, she reached down with her other hand and scooped him up.

"Mom, Maa-mou's never been at our house!" said Tess. "This is the only home he knows. Do you think he'll like it on shore?"

"Oh, I think he'll get used to it," said Sue. "And besides, he can always come out with me when you're in school."

Tess lifted him up to the roof of the wheelhouse, safely out of the way. He curled up inside a coil of rope, soaking up the morning sun and watching the gulls flying overhead.

"This is a good spot!" said Tess, bending over the gunwale with the gaff. "Hey, Mom, strike three! I think you better help me."

"Tess, you're catching more than I am!" Sue answered with a laugh as she left her line to help Tess pull in three fish, one on each hook. "You've sure learned a lot this summer," she said as she picked up the pliers to remove the hooks.

"Good teacher!" laughed Tess.

"Good student!" replied Sue.

Tess looked across the water to the nearby islands. The gnarled silver snags of old cedar trees were filled with the unmistakable shapes of eagles. Most were perched, unmoving except for their heads, which tilted from one side to the other, searching the sea below them. Others glided high on the air currents, slowly circling, their huge wings outstretched

"Mom! Look at all the eagles!"

Sue stood up. "They're waiting for the salmon to start up the rivers. By mid-August you always see lots of them around here."

"There must be at least twenty-five. I've never seen so many in one place before. That would make a great picture with a telephoto lens!" Tess paused. "Mom, if I spend some of my money on a camera, I could join the photo club when I go back to school. Then when we're back next summer I'd be able to take really good pictures."

"So you think you want to try another summer of fishing?" asked Sue in a teasing but pleased tone.

Tess grinned at her. "It's not as bad as I thought it would be." She was quiet for a moment. "I'm glad you fish. Not many kids get to see all the things I've seen this summer. Something else, Mom, I want to learn more about the ocean. There is so much to learn."

"Yes, it's another world under there," said Sue starting to warm up to one of her favourite topics. "I never get tired of learning about it. There is always something new to discover. We need to take care of it in the same way we need to take care of where we live. It's all connected, the ocean, the land, the air."

Suddenly the radiophone crackled to life.

"Mayday, Mayday, this is the *Lucky Strike*. We have engine trouble and are drifting off the east end of Numas Island."

"Listen, Tess. That's close to us." Sue left her line. "I'm going to call the Coast Guard," she said as she hurried into the wheelhouse.

"Coast Guard, Coast Guard. This is the *Henry Bay*."

"*Henry Bay*, this is the Coast Guard. Come in."

"We just heard the Mayday. I'm east off Numas Islands by Lewis Rocks. Do you want me to assist?"

"Thank you, *Henry Bay.* Yes, proceed to the site. We'll wait to hear from you."

"Okay, we're on our way."

Sue hung up the microphone and went back out on deck. Tess had already brought in her line and was starting on her mother's.

"Thanks, Tess," said Sue. "Well, I guess we have another job to do."

"*Henry* to the rescue!" said Tess, putting the gaffs away.

While Tess tidied up on deck, Sue headed into the wheelhouse to check the exact location of the boat in trouble. She measured the distance on the chart, turned on the radar, and sped up the engine. She scanned the horizon with the binoculars.

When Tess came in, Sue turned to her. "Tess, these swells are a bit big. We may not be able to tie up to the other boat. I might get you to take *Henry* if I need to go aboard to look at their engine."

"But, Mom, I've never steered *Henry* without you."

"Don't worry. We'll see what it's like when we get a bit closer. Here, take the binoculars and see if you can see the *Lucky Strike.*"

They kept motoring towards Numas Island. Soon Tess made out a little dot. "I think I see them," she said, passing the binoculars to Sue.

"That's where they should be," Sue said.

As they came closer to the *Lucky Strike,* Tess started to worry about the size of the swells. She knew how hard it was to tie two boats together when they were both bouncing around. She could see two people waiting on deck.

Sue slowed the boat as she came alongside the *Lucky Strike.* She yelled, "Looks like it's too rough to tie up. I'll come close and jump across. Get your fenders out." The man and the woman quickly put the bright orange balls over one side.

"Mom?" Tess turned to her with a worried look.

"You'll be okay," said Sue gently. "I won't be long. After I jump I want you to take *Henry* and pull away slowly. Go out about half-way to the island and then make slow circles around the *Lucky Strike* while you wait. I'll call when I'm done and will help guide you back."

"Mom, I'm scared."

"You can do it. Remember all the things you've been practising this summer. Go easy on the throttle. There's not much wind, just the swells to deal with. Now, take the wheel."

Tess took a deep breath. She put her hands firmly on the wheel. She planted her feet apart and squared her shoulders. Even though she didn't want to, Tess knew she had to help. And, right now, steering *Henry* was the only way she could. Sue gave her a quick hug and stepped onto the gunwale. She turned to her with a smile and a thumbs-up salute.

"That's my girl," Sue said, and jumped across to the other boat.

Panic surged through Tess. She was alone, alone on *Henry* for the first time in her life. It was all up to her. She pushed up the throttle and slowly pulled away from the *Lucky Strike.* She glanced over at the boat, aware that her mother was watching her. She waved and tried to look confident. Sue waved back, then disappeared below deck.

Tess steered *Henry* towards the island and began to make a big circle. She looked up at Maa-mou, who was sitting above her on the wheelhouse roof, looking down at her. Well, she wasn't completely alone.

"I don't like this, Maa-mou. What if I can't steer *Henry* back beside the boat?" Maa-mou started to wash his paw. "I hope Mom hurries up." Tess could hear the trembling in her voice.

She looked around anxiously. "The wind is starting to blow. It'll push *Henry* closer. I had better make another circle."

The minutes stretched on forever. "It's one thing to steer the boat out in open water," said Tess, "but what about getting back to the other boat?"

Maa-mou meowed his concern.

"What's taking Mom so long, Maa-mou?"

Maa-mou leaned his head over and stretched his paw down towards Tess's head. "I'm glad you're here, Maa-mou. I wouldn't want to be here all by myself."

She looked across at the *Lucky Strike.* She could see the three figures moving about on the deck. What were they doing? She looked at the rocky shore behind them. It seemed very close. Were they drifting in towards the shore?

"I can't make another circle," she said to Maa-mou. "I'll be too close to those rocks if I do."

She looked around wildly. Her palms were wet, her stomach knotted.

Then her mother's calm voice echoed in her head.

Remember everything you have learned this summer. Tess took a deep breath. She looked carefully at the *Lucky Strike*, the waves, and the wind indicator above her on the mast. She thought carefully of the things her mother had told her about winds and currents and drifting boats.

Again, she looked closely at the *Lucky Strike*. They couldn't have drifted in towards the rocks. The wind and the waves would be pushing them in the other direction. She turned *Henry*'s bow around. It was her fear and her imagination getting the best of her again. There was still plenty of room for her to make another circle.

As she brought *Henry* around again Tess saw two small dorsal fins break the surface just beyond her and disappear again. It happened so quickly that Tess wondered if she had been seeing things. But Maa-mou, too, was staring at the spot where the dolphins had disappeared.

Then the dolphins leaped out of the water again. They raced alongside the boat, but they kept their distance.

Tess smiled at Maa-mou. "They're looking after us," she said, feeling more confident. The dolphins cut across *Henry*'s bow, and then they were gone.

Tess glanced back at the *Lucky Strike* and saw her mother wave.

"Tess, come on over." Sue's voice was faint over the sound of the engine.

"About time!" said Tess with relief. Then she remembered what came next. "Now what do I do? I've got to steer *Henry* back to the other boat." She gulped. "Well,

Maa-mou, here goes nothing." She headed for the *Lucky Strike.*

Sue called to her again. This time her voice was louder and clearer. "Okay, Tess, now listen carefully. Keep coming closer. Take your time. Slow down as you turn. Give yourself lots of room to turn before you come alongside us."

Tess gripped the wheel. The distance between the boats was shrinking too fast. She pulled the throttle to stop, but *Henry* kept moving. She felt out of control. Above her panic she was vaguely aware of her mother's voice.

"Tess. That's too much. Speed up a bit. You need the speed for control. Now turn harder. No! The other way!"

Tess squeezed her eyes shut for a second. Visions of the boats crashing and sinking flashed through her mind. She quickly opened her eyes and spun the wheel in the opposite direction. "Now what do I do?" she called.

Sue's voice, strong and calm, cut through her fear. "You're too far out. Make another circle and come in again. A bit faster. Come up almost behind us."

Tess circled again. Maa-mou paced back and forth on the roof.

"I don't like this," Tess said with gritted teeth as she began to bring *Henry* into position to come alongside the *Lucky Strike.* Sue's voice continued calmly above the drone of the engine. "Good. Keep coming. A bit faster. That's it, now you've got it. Cut the throttle. Hold the wheel steady."

The two boats were almost side by side. Sue was

ready on the gunwale. "Good work, Tess!" She turned to the couple. "You should be okay until you get to the harbour."

Tess held her breath as the two boats touched. The fenders squeaked loudly as the boats bounced off each other. As Sue stepped across onto *Henry*'s deck, a big swell rolled the boats. Sue landed hard, staggered, and stopped herself from falling by grabbing the icebox.

"Mom, are you all right?"

"Yes, I think so," said Sue, leaning against the icebox. She waved to the couple.

The engine of the *Lucky Strike* rumbled as they pulled away. "Thanks, again," called the woman.

"Tess, you did just fine. I'm really proud of you," said Sue, slipping off her boot. "They were losing oil, but I was able to tighten up the gaskets. They'll have enough to get to Alert Bay where they can get their engine fixed properly."

Sue wiggled her toes and winced.

"Mom, what's wrong?" asked Tess, alarmed.

"I must have twisted my ankle when I jumped. It'll be fine in a minute." She bent over to pull off her sock. "How did it feel out there?"

"It was a bit scary," said Tess, thinking again of how small and alone she had felt on the vastness of the ocean, and how slowly the time had passed as she'd circled the *Lucky Strike.*

"I'm sure it was," said Sue.

"But I did it!" said Tess.

"You did. And you did it well," said Sue.

Tess was quiet for a moment. It had been scary, she wasn't going to deny that. But she had dealt with her fear and her imagination by using her head, by remembering and thinking exactly what she had to do. And Maa-mou had been with her. That had helped.

Tess smiled at Sue. It felt good to have done what she could do, and to make Mom proud. She felt a little bit bigger, and certainly a lot braver.

"Did you see the dolphins, Mom?"

"No, I didn't," said Sue "My head was in the engine most of the time."

"There were two of them, swimming really fast. We only saw them jump a few times and then they were gone. But I remembered what you said about dolphins making you feel safe. And they made me feel better, too."

"That's good," said Sue. "I know it was a hard thing to do, steering *Henry* all by yourself. You know, I wouldn't have asked you to do it if I didn't think that you could. It's another first for you, and often our fear makes it the hardest." Sue tried taking a step. She sucked in her breath, and grabbed hold of the door. Tess looked down at her mother's foot. The ankle was turning blue and swelling.

"I'll get you some ice," she said to Sue. She left the wheel and quickly scooped some ice out of the box. She dumped the ice into a plastic bag and followed her mother into the wheelhouse.

Tess took the wheel at the captain's chair. Sue propped up her leg and put the ice-pack on her foot. Maa-mou came in and sniffed at it. Sue was quiet for a long time. Tess kept glancing back at her, wondering what it was she was thinking.

Finally, Sue broke the silence. "It looks as if I've

sprained my ankle, Tess. I won't be able to do much like this. I guess we'll have to head home early."

Tess's hand tightened on the steering-wheel. She turned to her mother. She wasn't sure she understood.

"You mean, go back to Lund? What about fishing? We have two more weeks." Tess felt her mother's eyes on her. She turned away and looked ahead out the window. A long moment of silence passed between them.

Thoughts tumbled into Tess's head. The majesty of the orcas, the cry of the ravens, the shades of blues and purples of the islands at dusk. The rhythm of her day, the closeness between her and her mother on the boat. And even the hard work and the cold and the wet. That, too, was part of it. Part of her summer.

Suddenly she knew, more strongly than anything she'd ever known, that she wasn't ready for this summer to end. What had started out to be such hard, boring, and seemingly endless work, work that she had done only because her mother had wanted her to do it, had changed somewhere along the way. The change had been gradual. But she realized now that she had come to enjoy the work. And the work had become only a small part of all the other special things that had happened to her during the summer's trip. She realized how much she had come to like her life on the boat. Each day brought its new adventures and experiences, its new places and people. Tess knew she wasn't ready to go back to life on land. Not quite.

"No, Mom, we can't stop fishing. Not yet." Tess was surprised at the firmness in her own voice.

"Well, what else can we do? If I can't get around with this ankle—"

Tess was silent for a minute. She looked out the window and then back to her mother. She took a deep breath. "Mom, I've learned a lot this summer. You even said so. I can steer while you rest. I can even do more fishing."

"But—"

"Mom, it's only for another two weeks," said Tess. "I don't want to go home yet. Even if we don't catch as much."

"But, Tess, what about docking and unloading fish and all—"

"I can dock now. We can do it together. I know we can. You've taught me how. You'd be right there beside me. And your foot will get better soon. Please, Mom, let's try."

Sue sat quietly for a minute. She looked at Tess. "I guess we both have learned a lot this summer," she said. Maa-mou jumped up on her lap and began to purr. "Even you, you rascal," she said, scratching Maa-mou behind the ears.

Sue looked back at Tess, whose face was eager and excited. She thought of the morning in June when they had left Lund behind them. She remembered Tess's anger and frustration. Yes, a lot had happened this summer, to both of them. It was a summer of surprises, in more ways than she could ever have imagined. A slow smile spread across her face.

"Okay, Captain," she said. "We'll give it a try."

"All right, Mom!"

Tess sat tall in the captain's chair. Her hands rested easily on the wheel as she turned to look ahead. She pushed the throttle forward. The engine rumbled as

Henry dug her nose into the waves.

"You navigate, Mom, and I'll head for our next spot," said Tess. It was only three in the afternoon. They could fish for another hour or two. And then maybe Tess would make dinner. Right now, she felt like she could do everything.

Tess leaned back in the captain's chair. She reached out her foot towards the steering-wheel. It was a bit of a stretch. She sat up taller and tried again. She could just rest her toe on the rim of the wheel. She gave the wheel a gentle push. *Henry*'s nose turned. Tess smiled. Her mother sometimes steered *Henry* with her foot. Tess figured she was big enough, now, to give it a try.

About the Author

Jan Padgett is a writer and film-maker who lives in Powell River, B.C. She is a third generation West Coaster who comes from one of the pioneer families that settled the area. Jan has always lived on the coast, and has explored parts of it on fish boats and in her kayak, but it was a reunion with a school friend who owned and operated a classic live-hold fish boat called the *Henry Bay* that inspired her to write *The Reluctant Deckhand*.

Jan lives with her partner and her two daughters on a bank overlooking Georgia Strait. They share their place with a family of eagles, seals, deer, and bears, and many songbirds. They also have eight horses, a dog, a cat, two turtles, a large garden, and an orchard.

Jan has written several short stories about life on British Columbia's coastline. This is her first novel, a companion to the animated film of the same title that she wrote and directed. Jan is currently at work on her second novel.

Nautical and Fishing Terms Used in *The Reluctant Deckhand*

Anemone   A sea animal with petal-like tentacles of vibrant colours like green, pink, or purple. An anemone can be as small as a golfball or as big as a football.

Barge   A large, rectangular flat-bottomed craft, usually towed by a tug and used for transporting freight.

Boom   A series of connected, floating logs used to hold and tow other timber.

Bow   The front part of a boat or ship.

Breakwater   A barrier built of rocks or other materials that creates a sheltered harbour in a bay or cove.

Buoy   An anchored float that marks a navigable course or the location of a reef.

Channel   A wide passage of water between a continent and an island or between two islands.

Cod   A large food fish with a club-shaped head found in northern waters. See Lingcod.

Crabnet   A net lowered to sit on the ocean floor and used to catch crabs. Crabs enter the net through a trap door which closes behind them.

Echolocation The process by which the location of an object is determined by reflecting sounds off it.

Fender   A piece of old cable or a series of plastic balls hung over the side of a boat to protect it from impact.

Gasket   A flat sheet or ring of rubber which seals together two metal surfaces.

Galley	The kitchen of a ship.
Gaff	A strong hook with a handle used for landing large fish.
Gunwale	The upper edge of a ship's or a boat's side.
Halibut	Either of two large species of flatfish of the north Atlantic and the north Pacific.
Hatch	An opening in a ship's deck, or the cover for the opening.
Herring	A small fish living in large schools often used as bait to catch larger fish.
Hold	The interior of a ship below the deck where cargo is stored.
Hull	The frame or the body of a boat or a ship; the part that rests in the water.
Ice hold	The box on the stern of the boat in which ice is stored.
Inlet	A small arm of a sea, lake, or river.
Jigging	The action of pulling a fishing line up an arm's length and then letting the line drop into the water in such a way that the falling jig resembles an injured fish.
Lingcod	An elongated fish of the cod family with a greenish speckled body.
Mast	A long thin piece of wood or steel standing upright on a ship, that supports the sails or the rigging.
Mate	A person on a ship whose duties are to assist the captain or an officer or member of the crew. The first mate assists the captain directly.

Passage   A voyage across the sea from one port to another; or the way or route or channel through which a boat can pass.

Port   A city or town where ships can unload, or a safe harbour where ships can take refuge from a storm; also, the left side of a ship when one is facing the bow.

Pylon   A large upright timber that supports a dock or wharf.

Rapids   Fast-moving water; on the ocean caused by tidal currents pushing through narrow bits of land.

Reef   A ridge of rock or sand at or just below the surface of the ocean. Reefs are home to many different kinds of sea life.

Rockfish   A small fish with a prominent spine which lives on rocky bottoms. The many types of rockfish include red-banded, copper, dark-blotched, green-striped, yellow-tail, quill back, china, and tiger.

Scupper   A hole in a boat's side through which water streams off the deck.

Skipper   The captain of a small ship.

Snapper   A large fish with a bright reddish-orange body. Also called yelloweye rockfish.

Sound   A passage or channel of water between a mainland and an island or two connecting seas; or a relatively large inlet or arm of the sea or the ocean.

Southeaster   A wind from the southeast.

Starboard   The right-hand side of a ship when one is facing the bow.

Stern   The back end of a ship or boat.

Strait   A narrow passage of water connecting two larger bodies of water.

Tide   The rise and the fall of water in the ocean every twelve hours due to the gravitational pull of the sun and the moon.

Tug   A small strongly-built boat designed for pulling or pushing other vessels.

Wake   The track left by a ship moving through water.

Water-line   The line along which the surface of a body of water touches a ship's side.

Wet hold   The back section of the boat below deck filled with sea water in which live fish are kept. Water filters in and out of the hold through small holes in the boat's hull.

Wheelhouse   Shelter on a boat which contains the steering-wheel and from which the captain navigates the vessel.

Whirlpool   A circular current of water produced by the wind meeting tides or tidal currents.

Winch   A machine used to hoist or raise an object, comprised of a drum-shaped cylinder and a crank or handle with which to turn it.

The Reluctant Deckhand

The Reluctant Deckhand is available as a 33-minute animated film from the National Film Board, and can be purchased as a novel and videocassette package accompanied by a teacher's guide. The video includes interviews with the author, Jan Padgett, the animator, Amanda Forbis, and the owner of the *Henry Bay*, Sue Milligan. The teacher's guide, which shows how the package can be integrated into existing curricula, provides a wide range of activities and approaches to the novel and the film that will help students respond to the story in creative ways.

Other Children's Fiction from Pacific Educational Press

Gaetz, Dayle. *A Sea Lion Called Salena*
    For ages 8 to 11. ISBN 0-88865-069-8 $8.95

Haig-Brown, Alan. *The Suzie A*
    For ages 9 to 12. ISBN 0-88865-068-X $9.95

Horne, Constance. *The Jo Boy Deserts & Other Stories*
    For ages 7 to 10. ISBN 0-88865-085-X $7.95

———. *Trapped By Coal*
    For ages 8 to 11. ISBN 0-88865-091-4 $8.95

Walsh, Ann. *Moses, Me & Murder*
    For ages 7 to 10. ISBN 0-88865-059-0 $9.95

Pacific Educational Press, Faculty of Education, University of British Columbia, Vancouver, B.C., V6T 1Z4